I0583333
SAVING
This Song For You
BY BRITTANY N THOMAS

SAVING
This Song For You
BY BRITTANY N THOMAS

Manuscript Mistress

Saving (This Song For) You

Published by Manuscript Mistress, LLC
Jacksonville, Florida 32207 U.S.A

Edited by Manuscript Mistress, LLC / Brittany N. Thomas

Cover Designed by Manuscript Mistress, LLC / Brittany N. Thomas

Illustrations by Manuscript Mistress, LLC / Brittany N. Thomas

ISBN—979-8-9997016-0-2

First printing August 2025

Printed in the United States of America

All Scripture Quotations are from the Holy Bible. New Living Translation (NLT), New International Version (NIV), English Standard Version (ESV), and American Standard Version (ASV).

This book is a work of creative nonfiction. While all the stories in this book are true, they only serve as generalizations to some of our most common life experiences. Subject matter is solely for informational and motivational purposes. The strategies and advice presented in this book are not a substitute for professional counseling, therapy, or guidance. Seek guidance from qualified professionals for personalized support.

The author does not represent any company, corporation, or brand mentioned herein.

This book contains subject matter that could trigger emotional distress or discomfort for some readers. Reader discretion advised.

All names, characters, or incidents used are a product of the author's imagination. Any resemblance to actual persons, living or dead, is entirely coincidental. The views expressed in this collection are solely those of the authors.

For more information, contact ManuscriptMistress@icloud.com or visit www.manuscriptmistress.com

Dedication

First, I want to take a moment to say, **"Thank you, God!** Thank you for placing the idea for this book in my heart and mind. Thank you, Lord, for not allowing the vision to slip from my grasp, regardless of how many times I stalled in the creation of this book. No matter how often I said, "I'll start next week, next month, or even next year," the vision never diminished, and I am forever grateful for that.

Oftentimes, because we are disobedient in following what God tells us to do, he will strip us of those gifts and give them to someone else who is moving in obedience. So again, I say thank you for preserving this body of work specifically for me, especially since delayed obedience is still disobedience. Yet, God, you still covered my ideas amid my disobedience. For that, I am forever grateful. Of course, I wanted nothing more than for it to be perfect, as though I were what most would consider a perfectionist; however, since perfection is unattainable for me, I figured what better time than now to share your message through my methods and allow for its perfection through Christ Jesus.

Second, to my mother, my favorite girl. The one whom I affectionately call "Ma." You are so much more than what meets the eye, at least to me. You are my earth vessel (life giver), confidant, and friend. Thank you for pushing me past my limits. Oftentimes, you recognized my gifts and talents before I saw /recognized them as gifts and talents. With that said, thank you for pressing me to complete this book, no matter how much it got on my nerves or how many times I resisted due to imposter syndrome, for giving me the grace and the space when I asked for "yet another year extension," to your dismay, lol. Hopefully, you can rest assured that I have finally written the book. Now, you can't tell people I don't listen to you because this book proves that I hear you, value your opinion, and do what you say, even if I do it my way. Thank you. I love you with ALL of my being.

To my Father, my "Daddy"—the coolest, funniest, flyest, and most compassionate man I know—the "twin flame" behind my pen, "The Original Wordsmith or any other phrase I can use to describe the man behind my creative spark." In short, the perfect combination of God's Gift and YOUR way with words encapsulates my writing style. And I made sure to thank God first, so it's my turn to thank you, too.

And look at God; we're BOTH authors now :)

Furthermore, you taught me to do things at my own speed and not at the pace of others. You would repeatedly tell me, **"You are the only YOU! You are the only person with your fingerprints!"** You taught me early on the importance of being uniquely me and appreciating myself for exactly who God created me to be. And that would include tapping into my unique set of God-given skills. I love and appreciate you so much for that.

There are so many things that I can thank you both for, but in sum, I thank you both for your unwavering love and support in my childhood and beyond. Your support has been invaluable, and I love you both wholeheartedly!

Last but not least, I dedicate this book to **YOU**! And if you haven't heard it from anyone else, I want YOU to know that I love and value you and believe you are worthy of everything you want, need, and desire. Most importantly, you matter. You are unique, and your uniqueness is a gift to the world.

I hope you gain at least one thing from this body of work, even if it's just realizing that God loves YOU, too. And he loves you more than you'll ever know ;)

Intro

Music is a universal language. It transcends all races, languages, social barriers, and cultures. Because music is one of the most influential forms of media on this earth, I've realized that we can stay encouraged and steadfast in our salvation through song AND study.

On that note, this **"Book of Songs"** aims to bridge the gap between some of today's most popular inspirational songs from both contemporary and non-contemporary artists and the Word of God.

So, whether you are a starter in your faith, stagnant in your faith, or steady in your walk with Christ, we all need constant refreshers on who God is in our lives and what God can do for those of us who believe. And what better way to solidify God's message than with songs that stand as a testament to God's goodness, promises, and plan for your life?

PART ONE

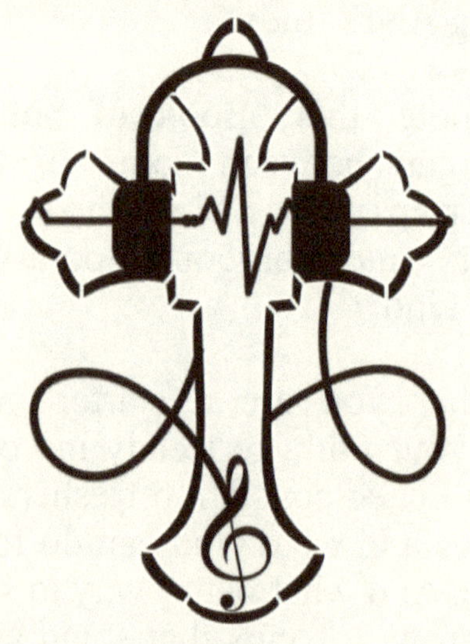

GOD IS...

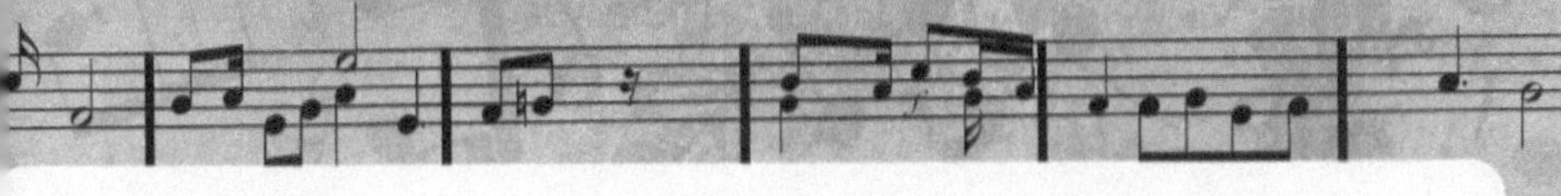

The Author & The Finisher of Our Lives

Verses

"This is what the Lord says: "When seventy years are completed for Babylon, I will come to you and fulfill my good promise to bring you back to this place. For I know the plans I have for you," declares the Lord, "plans to prosper you and not to harm you, plans to give you hope and a future. Then you will call on me and come and pray to me, and I will listen to you. You will seek me and find me when you seek me with all your heart. I will be found by you," declares the Lord, "and will bring you back from captivity. I will gather you from all the nations and places where I have banished you," declares the Lord, "and will bring you back to the place from which I carried you into exile."

Jeremiah 29:10-14 NIV

Have you ever gone to a friend's vision board party and hoped, and prayed with all of your heart, that each of those pictures you so strategically cut out and glued to your board would become a part of your reality within the next twenty-four hours or less, regardless of whether it was in God's will for you or not? Or, as a youth, did you envision yourself to be married with children by twenty-five years of age, only for you to be currently overage, single, and childless? What about imagining that you would land your dream job by thirty-five, only to end up thirty-five and unemployed?

On the contrary, have you ever prayed to God for healing, and within no time, it was as if you were never sick? One minute, the doctors are telling you that they found a spot on your liver, and by the next visit, there's not a spot in sight. How about praying for reconciliation with a former friend or a family member, maybe even an ex, and years later, no one can tell it was a disconnect in the relationship? Lastly, have you ever believed in God for that dream house or car, and before you knew it, you had everything you wanted?

Believe it or not, if you answered "yes" to any of these questions, you are likely overstepping and/or potentially interjecting yourself into God's already perfect plan for your life. As a result, you could become the root cause of your downfall. How, you ask? **Proverbs 19:21 NIV** says, "Many are the plans in a person's heart, but the Lord's purpose prevails." In other words, God knows that we will have many plans for ourselves, but ultimately, whether or not those plans come to fruition is in God's hands, not ours.

Now, do not be dismayed, as God does want us to both have AND work towards goals because, as we all know, faith without works is DEAD (**James 2:18-26 NIV**). So, please know that it's okay for us to have earthly desires and believe in God for everything we want. Still, we must also realize that we can pray all day long, but without putting in the sweat equity behind those prayers AND waiting for God's response and alignment, our request to God can often be in vain.

You may be asking, well, what does that mean to me? To put it plainly, you must reach a point where you relinquish yourself and your plans for your life to God and completely trust in God's plan for you. We often spend our precious time obsessing over every little thing. We constantly worry about how things will unfold in our personal lives, family life, careers, and countless other things beyond our control. However, everything we experience in our lives, whether good or bad, the creator has already predestined each of those things to occur, both for us and through us.

Suppose you are anything like me and need additional scripture to support those claims. In that case, **Ephesians 1:11-14 NIV** says, "In him we were also chosen, having been predestined according to the plan of him who works out everything in conformity with the purpose of his will. So that we, who were the first to put our hope in Christ, might be for the praise of his glory. And you also were included in Christ when you heard the message of truth, the gospel of your salvation. When you believed, you were marked in him with a seal, the promised Holy Spirit, a deposit guaranteeing our inheritance until the redemption of those who are God's possession to the praise of his glory." That passage tells us that God had already written our every experience in his will. And just like I am the author of this book and have carefully crafted the beginning, middle, and end of this text, God has done the same for you. He knows your story from the beginning of your life until your last day. " So when you can't see what tomorrow holds, and yesterday is through, remember HE knows his plans for you." Rest assured that you do not have to figure anything out, because God has already done the legwork for you.

Notes

"Sing to the Lord a new song; sing to the Lord, all the earth. Sing to the Lord, praise his name; Proclaim his salvation day after day. Declare his glory among the nations, his marvelous deeds among all people. For great is the Lord, and most worthy of praise; he is to be feared above all God's"

-Psalms 96:1-4 NIV

Notes

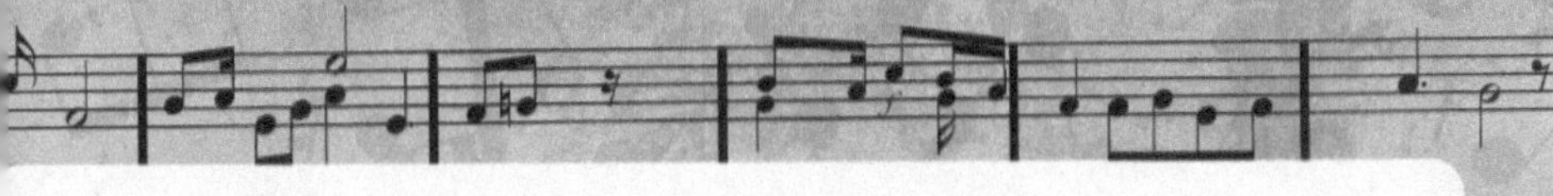

The Ultimate Parent

Verses

"In your struggle against sin, you have not yet resisted to the point of shedding your blood. And have you completely forgotten this word of encouragement that addresses you as a father addresses his son? It says, "My son, do not make light of the Lord's discipline, and do not lose heart when he rebukes you, because the Lord disciplines the one he loves, and he chastens everyone he accepts as his son." Endure hardship as discipline; God is treating you as his children. For what children are not disciplined by their father? If you are not disciplined—and everyone undergoes discipline—then you are not legitimate, not true sons and daughters at all. Moreover, we have all had human fathers who disciplined us and we respected them for it. How much more should we submit to the Father of spirits and live! They disciplined us for a little while as they thought best; but God disciplines us for our good, in order that we may share in his holiness. No discipline seems pleasant at the time, but painful. Later on, however, it produces a harvest of righteousness and peace for those who have been trained by it. Therefore, strengthen your feeble arms and weak knees. Make level paths for your feet," so that the lame may not be disabled, but rather healed."

Hebrews 12:4-13 NIV

I like to refer to God as our ultimate parent. Why, you ask? Envision this: just as your parent(s) / guardian(s) ensured you always had everything you wanted and needed in their care, God wants you to have everything you want and need in him. Your parents withheld nothing, from unlimited love, safety, and guidance to shelter, clothes, and shoes. You always had your favorite foods, drinks, and snacks whenever you wanted them. Reflect on the joy you felt when you were rewarded with your favorite toys, gaming systems, or even jewels when you did as instructed; that is the exact feeling times infinity you'll get when God is involved in your daily life.

Realistically, we know that not every facet of the parent-child relationship is always joyous. For example, when you were disobedient to your parent, you suffered the consequences of your actions. Like when you stole your mom's car and went on a joy ride? Please think of how you felt when she reported the vehicle stolen, despite knowing that you were the culprit, or recall the night you snuck out of your bedroom window. You went to that party your parents forbade [1] you from going to, only to return home after a fun night, and your parents were waiting for you by the door. That reprimand was memorable, right? But regardless of how much you hated being punished at the moment, looking back, you likely realize

---

[1] Forbade: to refuse to allow something / Order someone not to do something

there's a lesson in the stress. Your parents often do everything in their power to keep you alive and well until you're old enough to think and care for yourself. And although it doesn't seem like it, you are only corrected to ensure you are rooted in respect for authority and grounded in discipline. Reprimanding is not always hatred; instead, it provides an understanding of the importance of following directions. A reprimand is in place to ensure you become your best self. Realistically, you can't make it through your daily routine without some form of discipline. For instance, it takes discipline to make it to work or school on time every day: to work an eight-hour shift, to make good on a prior commitment, and even to walk side by side with Christ. Sound familiar? Of course, it does.

God provides everything you require, but to access all of the "perks," you must fully subscribe to the lifestyle. Just as your parents expect you to comply while you're in their care and follow the rules they set forth, God is the same. The first step in walking with Christ is to believe in him and his plan for your life wholeheartedly, and second, and most importantly, you MUST do what he instructs you to do, regardless of whether it's favorable to you.

Just as an earthly parent punishes you when you don't follow directions, God treats us as his children (read **1 John 3:1-10 NIV**) and punishes us just the same (read **Revelation 3:19 NIV**).

Remember that, most times, discouragement from not earning that promotion on your job or not landing that promising contract you'd hoped for is a test you must endure before you reach your next level. However, it's important to note that God's denial can also result from your noncompliance.

For instance, say God tells you to sow your last fifty dollars to the stranger you walked past in the grocery store parking lot. However, instead of doing so and trusting that God will provide double for your trouble, you decide that you're going to be selfish and keep the money for yourself. Maybe you judged them, saying something like, *"They look well put together; they probably have more money than I do,"* not knowing that they just lost their job and that was your assignment to bless them (read **Hebrews 13:16 NIV**). Or maybe you questioned God, asking him, *"God, why would you ask me to give my last? How am I going to make it the rest of this week?"* Not realizing that at your next destination, God would use someone else to bless you with more money than you lost. Now, envision getting in your car, and the karma from your neglect comes instantly; for example, you catch a flat as you pull out of the parking lot. Or, karma may come when you least expect it, sometimes days, months, or even years after the disobedience occurs. So keep in mind that Father always Knows Best. When God asks you to do something, do it immediately because it's either a blessing or a lesson on the other side. **Choose wisely.**

Another thing that makes God the ultimate parent is that he is no respecter of persons. For example, say the entire first half of this section doesn't relate to you. Maybe you don't know what it's like to have the rearing, love, and shelter of a parent or guardian. Perhaps you were orphaned as a youth, so you didn't have the support that your peers had. Or maybe your earthly parents abandoned you for whatever reason, whether it be personal struggles like addiction, mental illness, or detachment. You may be thinking that God has forsaken you. But the beautiful thing about God is that he is a **Father to the Fatherless** (read **Psalm 68:5-6 NIV**), too. Please note, I do not believe that this is gender specific. It is my interpretation that God is simply a parent to the parentless. It is not a one-sided male or female thing, especially since we know God is omnipresent[2] and omnibenevolent.[3] In other words, God is everything to those who need him and is everywhere simultaneously. The Bible says, "You, Lord, hear the desire of the afflicted; you encourage them, and you listen to their cry, defending the fatherless and the oppressed so that mere earthly mortals will never again strike terror" **(Psalms 10:17-18 NIV).**

In sum, even though those of you who lacked parental guidance on earth have unlimited access

---

[2] Omnipresent in this context means everywhere at the same time

[3] Omnibenevolent in this context means all-loving

to God the Father every step of the way. And even when you feel alone, he's there, and he will never let you go. So, for those of you who have a parental void, have you ever wondered how you persevered with all the odds stacked against you? People counted you out and said you were cold and unable to love; you constantly carried the parent wound around everywhere you went, but you still held your head high, suffered, clawed, and stood. The short answer is God. He has his hands on you, hears your cries, and encourages you to keep going. He sees you, and he loves you, child. After all, that's what fathers do! So, you may not have had the support you wanted from wo(man), but remember this: God is all the father, the guardian you need, and you will find peace and belonging in him when you surrender.

Notes

"Sing to God, sing in praise of his name, extol him who rides
on the clouds; rejoice before him—his name is the Lord."

-Psalms 68:4 NIV

Notes

"Sing to God, sing in praise of his name, extol him who rides
on the clouds; rejoice before him—his name is the Lord."

-Psalms 68:4 NIV

Not A Man That He Should Lie

Verses

"God is not human, that he should lie, not a human being, that he should change his mind. Does he speak and then not act? Does he promise and not fulfill? I have received a command to bless; he has blessed, and I cannot change it. "No misfortune is seen in Jacob, no misery observed in Israel. The Lord their God is with them; the shout of the King is among them. God brought them out of Egypt; they have the strength of a wild ox. There is no divination against Jacob, no evil omens against Israel. It will now be said of Jacob and of Israel, 'See what God has done!' The people rise like a lioness; they rouse themselves like a lion that does not rest till it devours its prey and drinks the blood of its victims." Then Balak said to Balaam, "Neither curse them at all nor bless them at all!" Balaam answered, "Did I not tell you I must do whatever the Lord says?"

Numbers 23:19-26 NIV

Being set up for a letdown is never ideal, regardless of the reason. For instance, as a kid, did your parent(s) promise they would take you to Chuck E. Cheese over the weekend if you were good at school during the week, just for the weekend to get here, and they were "too tired" to take you? Or maybe your brother asked you to borrow $100 until payday, and payday came and went a few times over without a sign of repayment. You were fuming as you watched him flex[4] money on Instagram and purchase new clothes and shoes, yet he played the victim when you asked to be refunded. Have you ever been stood up by a potential suitor on a first date? Or did your "friends" purposely not show up for your birthday party, knowing you paid out of pocket to reserve their spot at the venue? Lastly, have you ever coordinated a trip for everyone to back out at the last minute once payments are due?

Simply put, have you ever been promised something, and the other party dropped the ball when the time came? Or what about you? Have you ever told someone you would do something and didn't hold up your end of the bargain? Even if you did not intend to do so? These are all examples of how easily men and women lie. And how we do so without a second thought. "Little white lies" or half-truths are how we deduce them. Instead of calling them what they are, **Bold Face Lies.**

---

[4] The term "flex" in this context is informal language / slang for being boastful or showing off

The irony in the human experience is that we hate being lied to, yet we spew out untruths daily. We lie to our children to "protect" them, saying things such as, "They're too young to understand," when all we have to do is meet them where they are by talking to them in a way they'll comprehend. Or, "Now is not the time," when there will never be a right time for the truth. In addition, we lie to our children to "deflect[5]" them, for instance, the Chuck E. Cheese example I used previously. As a parent, you'll say anything to silence the child(ren), even if it means faking a reward to keep them quiet, without realizing that you're not a person of your word. But that's not all; we often lie out of fear and disappointment to our parents, guardians, or persons of authority. We fear the consequences that may arise and the frustration associated with letting them down. And to others, we may lie out of safety. For example, we lie to protect ourselves or something sacred (i.e., lying out of fear that someone will spread false narratives/gossip).

But imagine if God did the same thing to you when you called on him. How would you feel? Picture this: you pray to God, and he makes you a blank promise. You know in your heart that God told you that you would have a breakthrough on Friday, and then Friday comes, and nothing happens. Imagine God boastfully gave your financial blessing to someone else when he

---

[5] Deflect: cause someone to deviate from the intended purpose / cause something to change direction by interposing (to intervene with) something

promised it was yours. Finally, what if God lied to you out of safety? Would you be mad at God? If your answer is yes, I think you should take some time to reevaluate how quickly you speak to others with bad intentions. God knows that we are not perfect people. However, he wants us to live as Christ-like as possible. A great place to start is by being honest with yourself and others. If you say you will do something, be intentional about it. Vice versa, if you've made up your mind that you're not going to do something, stand firm in that decision as well.

For those of you who say, *"Well, I am not a liar; I do my best to walk in truth and to be a great person, and I still feel as if I cry and pray to no avail. I feel as if God has forsaken me."* This passage is for you. "I assure you before God that what I am writing is no lie" **(Galatians 1:20 NIV).** You never have to worry about God going back on anything that he promised you. If God said it, it would come to pass. As God is not a man, he should not lie. However, we must remain patient and know God's timing is not ours. Years to humanity are the nick of time for God. So, we must remain vigilantly[6] hopeful while waiting for God's promises, for they will manifest themselves in due time. In short, just because what you believe in hasn't happened yet doesn't mean it won't. It just means God is taking extra time to ensure that everything you desire is everything you imagined.

---

[6] In this context, the term "vigilant" refers to "keeping careful watch / being watchful and hopeful."

Don't give up; rest assured that everything you want is on the other side of your waiting. But you must believe that YOU deserve what you're waiting for. And you must stand on the fact that God never lies to anyone, especially those he loves and cares for. If God said it, it is so! There are no ifs, ands, or buts about it (read **1 Samuel 15:29 NIV**).

Notes

"Sing to him, sing praise to him; tell of all his wonderful acts."

-1 Chronicles 16:9 NIV

Notes

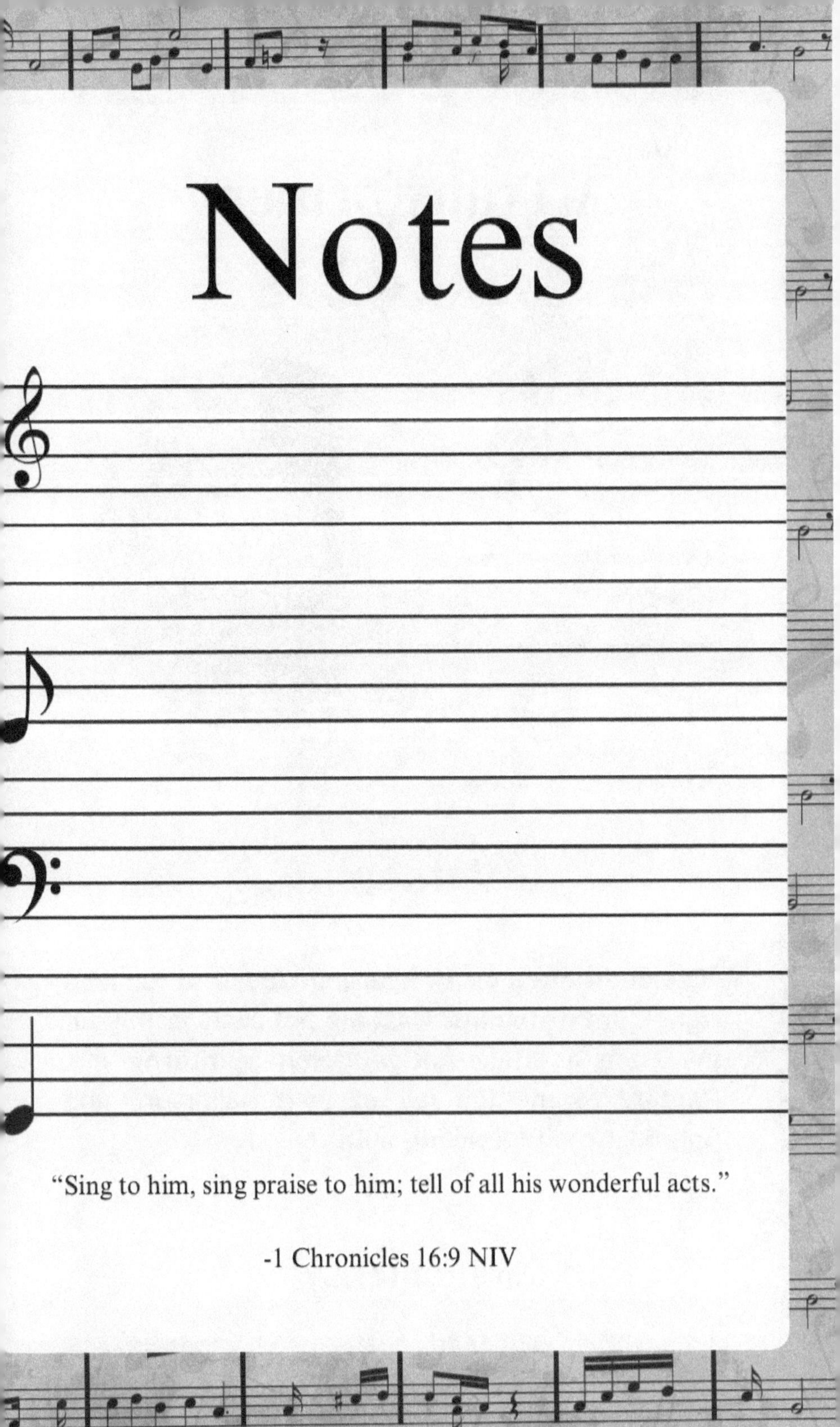

"Sing to him, sing praise to him; tell of all his wonderful acts."
-1 Chronicles 16:9 NIV

A Transformer

Verses

"Create in me a clean heart, O God, and renew a right spirit within me. Cast me not away from your presence, and take not your Holy Spirit from me. Restore to me the joy of your salvation, and uphold me with a willing spirit."

Psalm 51:10-12 ESV

Most people have the notion that we must be perfect before we decide to walk with Christ. However, that is far from the truth. In all actuality, God gains the most glory from your story when you choose to walk with him just as you are. God is not looking for perfection before acceptance, as most would assume. Instead, in your acceptance is where God does his perfecting. For instance, how often have you heard, "I have to get myself together first before I step foot inside the church again," or "I'll become more faithful in my prayer life once I can stop making silly mistakes. God doesn't want to hear from me if I'm going to do something wrong after I pray anyway." However, saying this is stalling God's opportunity for a breakthrough in your life.

An important thing to know about walking with God is that God is careful in crafting, yet jealous (read **Deuteronomy 4:24 NIV**). To elaborate further, God knows what to do to change and perfect you, but he needs your undivided devotion and attention. God will not share you with the world. You must choose a side. You're either for God or against God. There's no such thing as in-between (read **Revelation 3:14-16 NIV**).

I don't intend to reduce God by any means, but in this instance, I think of God like a child who gets upset when you refuse to watch them do the new cartwheel trick they learned in gymnastics lessons. No matter how often you've seen them do this trick, they will still distance themselves, turn their backs, and fold their arms in disgust whenever they feel you're not paying proper attention to them. God is the same. Not in the sense that he will turn his back on us, because God never turns his back on those who believe. Instead, I am alluding to the idea that God will back off whenever we stray from him. If God sees our attention elsewhere, he will let us be until WE decide to re-approach him.

Furthermore, just like the cartwheel you've seen one thousand times, we, as the body of Christ (read **1 Corinthians 12:12-27 NIV**), have seen God routinely do the impossible in our lives, yet we still flee from him and resist his transformation. We focus on what we are missing out on, worldly pleasures and temporary means of satisfaction, instead of focusing on our one trustworthy source, God. Our resistance makes God very upset. However, as I stated, he will not fight for our attention. How does this show up, you may ask? Well, God will often appear stagnant or slow to answer our prayers. He will appear to give us the silent treatment as if he doesn't hear our cries, and will be seemingly distant. However, whenever you feel that way, **please know it is a YOU problem, not a God problem.** Because, as you know, we as humans tend to get in the way of our growth. So, whenever God feels "quiet" in your life, that indicates that God is either up to something good or is likely waiting for you to obey and accept your transition. He listens to you and sees you, but still wants you to make the first move. Remember, in the previous section, I mentioned that God is our ultimate parent. In the same way, your parent can "wash their hands with you"[7] and still love and protect you; your heavenly father treats you the same. He will let you go just so that you'll realize that in him is the only place you will attain perfect peace (Read **Isaiah 26:3 NIV**), and fundamental transformation will occur (read **Matthew 18:1-4 NIV**).

But please realize that true transformation starts with accepting Christ as the Lord and head of your life. Once you do so, it will lead you to the perfection you're striving for. In him, you will be made perfect. However, to attain the Lord's favor, you must come to him with expectations in your heart. You must seek and ask him to go into your heart and change you for his glory. At that point, God will begin making all your *"crooked paths straight"* (read **Proverbs 21:7-8 NIV**), but he will only start the process when YOU let him in. He will not force his way into your life; you have to open the door to your heart and let him in. God does it this way because God wants full credit for your transformation, not partial. In other words,

---

[7] Washing your hands in this context is a colloquialism and/or a phrase meant to explain a parent's ability to disapprove of what their child is doing; however, they still love and support their child while also giving them the space they need to grow and navigate their situation alone / without typical parental intervention, basically, when a parent allows a child to figure out a problem independently.

we often try to step in and do the work for God. However, he does not need our help, for he is God and God alone (read **Isaiah 45:5-25 NIV**). Instead, he needs our complete submission to prepare us for total transformation.

For instance, have you ever had that *"I know that was nobody but God"* type of moment? If you said yes, then you already know that God is an expert in the blessing business. He can do all things, but to receive God's things, you must do what he tells you to do. And you must back up when he tells you to. In addition, when you ask God for transformation, you must be ready to accept everything that comes with his transformation of your life. You cannot be afraid to acknowledge God in your heart or be scared to lose things that hinder your development. Because let's face it, when you ask God to show up as a transformer, things will begin to fall from your grasp. You will lose valuable connections, friends, romantic relationships, and many things you adore. It won't feel like anything good is happening; however, whenever things appear to be falling apart, it is usually when better things are on the horizon. So, stay encouraged and allow yourself to become a willing participant in your change by allowing God to step in so you can "Rid yourselves of all the offenses you have committed, and get a new heart and a new spirit." (read **Ezekiel 18:31 NIV**)

Notes

"Sing praises to God, sing praises; sing praises to our King, sing praises."

-Psalms 47:6 NIV

Notes

"Sing praises to God, sing praises; sing praises to our King, sing praises."

-Psalms 47:6 NIV

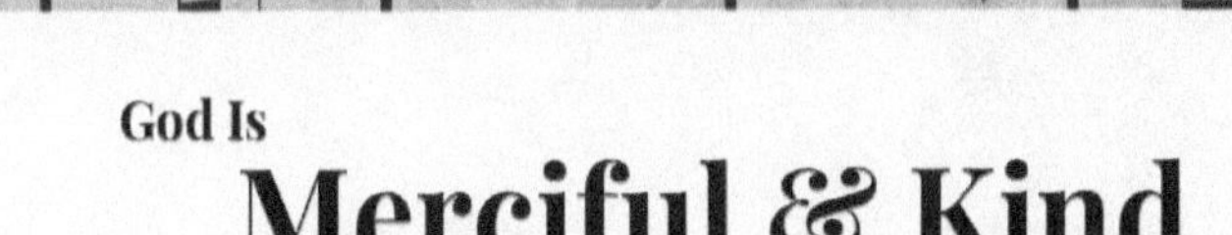

Verses

"And the Lord said to Moses, "This very thing that you have spoken I will do, for you have found favor in my sight, and I know you by name." Moses said, "Please show me your glory." And he said, "I will make all my goodness pass before you and will proclaim before you my name 'The Lord.' And I will be gracious to whom I will be gracious, and will show mercy on whom I will show mercy." (Exodus 33:17-19)

"For we do not have a high priest who is unable to sympathize with our weaknesses, but one who in every respect has been tempted as we are, yet without sin. Let us then with confidence draw near to the throne of grace, that we may receive mercy and find grace to help in time of need." (Hebrews 4:15-16 ESV)

"The steadfast love of the Lord never ceases; his mercies never come to an end; they are new every morning; great is your faithfulness. "The Lord is my portion," says my soul, "therefore I will hope in him." (Lamentations 3:22-24 ESV)

***Bonus Track: Amazing Grace - Ruben Studdard**

Being **Merciful** is showing or exercising compassion and/or relieving someone from something unpleasant. I decided to start with the definition because I feel most people don't comprehend what it means for God to be merciful. Instead, we fear the Lord, as we should (read **Ecclesiastes 5:4-7 NIV)**; however, that fear of God becomes so crippling that, most times, it hinders our notion of how kind and understanding God is.

Of course, when most Christians think about mercy, the ultimate example is the Crucifixion of Christ Jesus, who was sacrificed on Calvary to make us new each day (read **Luke 9:21-24 NIV & Galatians 2:15-21 NIV)**. That is mercy to the extreme. God relieved us of our unpleasantness through Jesus' sacrifice. I don't know about you, but only strong people can sacrifice their flesh and blood for someone else's gain. And whether you're a parent or not, I highly doubt you would sacrifice your child or a loved one for a group of ungrateful strangers.

However, although that is the most common example, it is not the only thing that makes God merciful. For instance, say you struggled with a drug addiction from the ages of thirteen to twenty-seven. You borrowed money you never intended to return, stole from friends, family, and strangers alike to get your fix, and wreaked havoc on anyone in the way of your habit. Eventually, friends and family loosened their grip; you spiraled out of control, lost your way, and felt you had no one to whom you could turn. Fast-forward to now, and you've been clean and sober for five years. And, while a few people decided to ignore your past transgressions, realistically, most people still held the mistakes of your past over your head. With each passing year, it seems you are taking one step forward, yet your past still binds you.

To further elaborate, say, at a family gathering, you run into a disgruntled aunt who was a victim of your addiction. As soon as you two lock your eyes, she snickers, then says, "Oh, let me go hide my purse now before you steal all my money," and hurriedly walks off. It takes everything in you to hold it together. You ask yourself, *"When will they understand I'm not that person anymore? That was the addiction, not ME. I'm doing all I can to walk on the straight and narrow. I even paid her back the money I stole from her, plus interest, over two years ago. She still won't let it go!"* You see, man[8] harbors and keeps a record of your offenses, just like your aunt who keeps you chained to your addiction. However, God does not. The beauty of God's mercy is that once we repent for our wrongdoings and actively pursue a life with Christ as the leader, he will throw ALL our sins into the sea of forgetfulness (read **Micah 7:19 NIV**). In other words, God will no longer remember the things of your past, no matter what you've done.

---

[8] The term "man" in this context is not gender specific.

Regardless of how bad, once you repent AND turn towards God, the blood of Jesus will wash you white as snow (read **Isaiah 1:18 NIV**).

Of course, I realize that not all examples are one-size-fits-all. So, let me take another route. Maybe you're not entangled by the chains of addiction, but perhaps you fought and cut ties with a friend or family member. During your idle time from one another, you found out that they were diagnosed with an aggressive form of Cancer. Typically, you're the type to hold grudges for months, maybe even years, but this time it's different. There's something inside of you telling you to step in. Usually, your stubborn demeanor would cause you to put up a wall and drown out God's voice. You'd make up excuses like, *"They wronged me; why must I be the bigger person? Don't get me wrong, I don't want anything to happen to them, I truly hate that they're sick, but I'm human too. I have feelings, too!"* But again, this time, it's different. Instead of resisting per usual, you obey God's voice and begin going to their house regularly, taking them food and other essentials such as medications, and doing so without complaint or mention of the original offense. You are there every step of the way, from taking them to appointments after the initial diagnosis to cheering them on as they ring the bell of freedom. Essentially, the once severed relationship was literally "nursed" back to health due to your compassion during their time of need. Being supportive of someone despite their shortcomings perfectly displays what mercy and kindness look like. Regardless of how much time has passed since the falling out, deciding to step in when someone needs you the most, without holding anything over their head, is exactly what God wants us to do for others, because that's what God does for us. Can you imagine your life if God decided not to be as merciful as he's been towards you? Where would you be without God's grace?

Take time to marinate on the above examples and reflect on how merciful and kind God has to be to forgive a wretch[9] like me and you (read **Romans 7:14-25 NIV**). To know that nothing you've ever done, said, or even imagined can withhold God's kindness from surrounding you. And if you're anything like me, you're probably thinking, *"Are you sure? I've done, said, or thought some pretty outlandish things."* The short answer is "yes." I'm more than sure. GREAT is God's Mercy and kindness towards us all day after day!

---

[9] A wretch is defined as a person who is in either a very unhappy or unfortunate state of being.

Notes

"Sing to God, you kingdoms of the earth, sing praise to the Lord,"

-Psalms 68:32 NIV

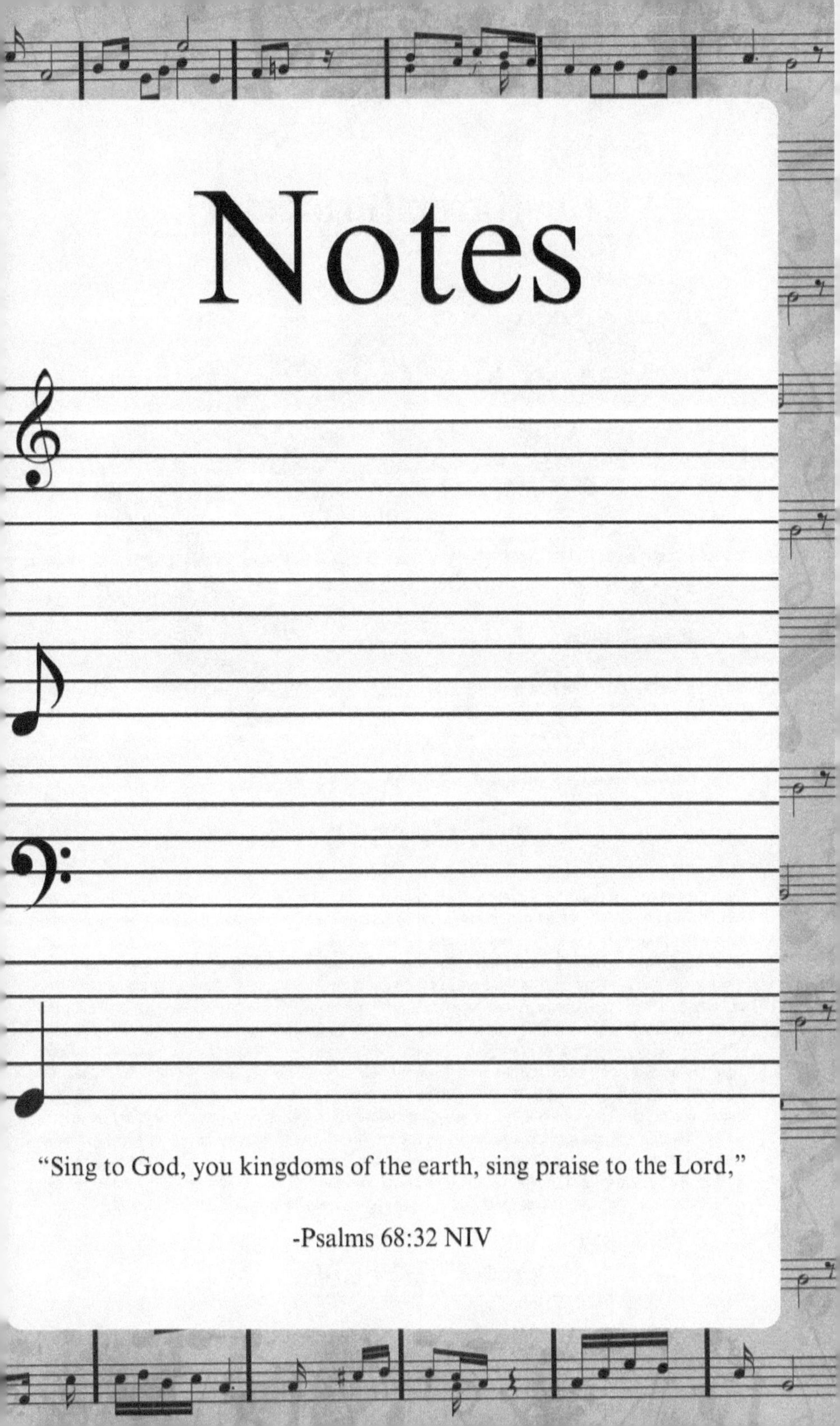

Notes

"Sing to God, you kingdoms of the earth, sing praise to the Lord,"

-Psalms 68:32 NIV

God Is

A Safe-Haven (Protector)

Verses

"The Lord is my light and my salvation— whom shall I fear? The Lord is the stronghold of my life— of whom shall I be afraid? When the wicked advance against me to devour me, it is my enemies and my foes who will stumble and fall. Though an army besiege me, my heart will not fear; though war break out against me, even then I will be confident. One thing I ask from the Lord, this only do I seek: that I may dwell in the house of the Lord all the days of my life, to gaze on the beauty of the Lord and to seek him in his temple. For in the day of trouble he will keep me safe in his dwelling; he will hide me in the shelter of his sacred tent and set me high upon a rock. Then my head will be exalted above the enemies who surround me; at his sacred tent I will sacrifice with shouts of joy; I will sing and make music to the Lord. Hear my voice when I call, Lord; be merciful to me and answer me. My heart says of you, "Seek his face!" Your face, Lord, I will seek. Do not hide your face from me, do not turn your servant away in anger; you have been my helper. Do not reject me or forsake me, God my Savior. Though my father and mother forsake me, the Lord will receive me. Teach me your way, Lord; lead me in a straight path because of my oppressors. Do not turn me over to the desire of my foes, for false witnesses rise up against me, spouting malicious accusations. I remain confident of this: I will see the goodness of the Lord in the land of the living. Wait for the Lord; be strong and take heart and wait for the Lord."

Psalms 27:1-14 NIV

Whether we like it or not, we all must work in some capacity.

In using a work-related example, say you've been looking for a job for months on end to no avail, and finally, you receive a callback. You beam with excitement at the shot to have gainful employment again. Normally, you clam up at the thought of an interview, but you're calm and confident this time, so much so that you can ace the interview in the first round.

Fast-forward to the present day. You go to work faithfully, never missing a day, showing up on time, and exceeding your company's expectations. However, it's not about them. It's bigger than the company. Instead, it's solely about walking in gratefulness to God for providing you with employment again. The Bible says, "Whatever you do, work at it with all your heart, as working for the Lord, not for human masters" (**Colossians 3:23 NIV**). And you are the embodiment of that verse. So much so, accolades are flying at you left and right, and you feel a sense of pride, faith, and confidence in your role.

You transitioned from not knowing where your next meal would come from to having a successful home, personal, and professional life. You essentially have it all. But there's only one problem: Your new boss has an apparent vendetta against you, so evident that other team members and colleagues take notice. You often contemplate reporting the issue; a few of your closest teammates even offered to report him so you could remain anonymous. However, you fear this will cause even more intimidation and threats from him and even eventual termination. And you've come too far to lose everything you've worked so hard to attain. Yet, although you're a bit shaken up at the thought of someone you work with so closely, and management at that, trying to sabotage you, you decide to remain calm. Instead of making a big deal in the workplace, you rely on God, take it to him in prayer, and change your heart posture. For instance, you stopped gossiping about it all day and poured your heart into your work. You decide to show up and perform your job duties as if no odds are against you. And after a few weeks of prayer, a sense of calm overwhelms you.

The weeks roll by, and the attacks don't stop. However, you're still unfazed. You know God's got your back. And good thing you are, because unbeknownst to you and your manager, his boss makes a surprise visit to the office and oversees him mistreating you, but this time, it's the worst it's ever been. She immediately reprimands him on the spot for his mistreatment of you, and because he's caught off guard, he tries to play it cool, but his efforts are in vain. He gets called into his office immediately. And when she enters his office, she unveils a trail of false claims against you, email threads with your manager gossiping about you, and more. The crazy thing is that everything was in plain sight; he didn't even try to hide it. She brings in reinforcement, pulling people aside and asking any colleagues in the area familiar with you to vouch for you and your character. She begins studying your track record for key factors such as quality and production rates, employee recognition, experience level, etc. Of course, you have plenty of good to show for it. After enough research, she decided to build a case against your manager. For the time being, until she gathered enough evidence, she decided to demote your manager, move him to a different area, and promote you to his position.

Talk about God's favor! In sum, keeping your focus on the job and not allowing negativity to seep into your heart helped to lay the groundwork for your promotion. God exalted you above the very enemy who tried to destroy you. That's the beautiful thing about God's presence in your life. He will protect you from all harm when you stay focused on him, not the attacks. Let's face it: attacks will come when you're a believer, but if you stand firm, the reward will always be greater than the adversity. For instance, God will often catapult you to a level unreachable by those who attacked you, but you must maintain your confidence in him. Remember, you will see the goodness of the Lord, but it all starts with your belief.

Notes

"I will sing to the Lord as long as I live; I will sing praise to my God while I have being."

-Psalm 104:33 ESV

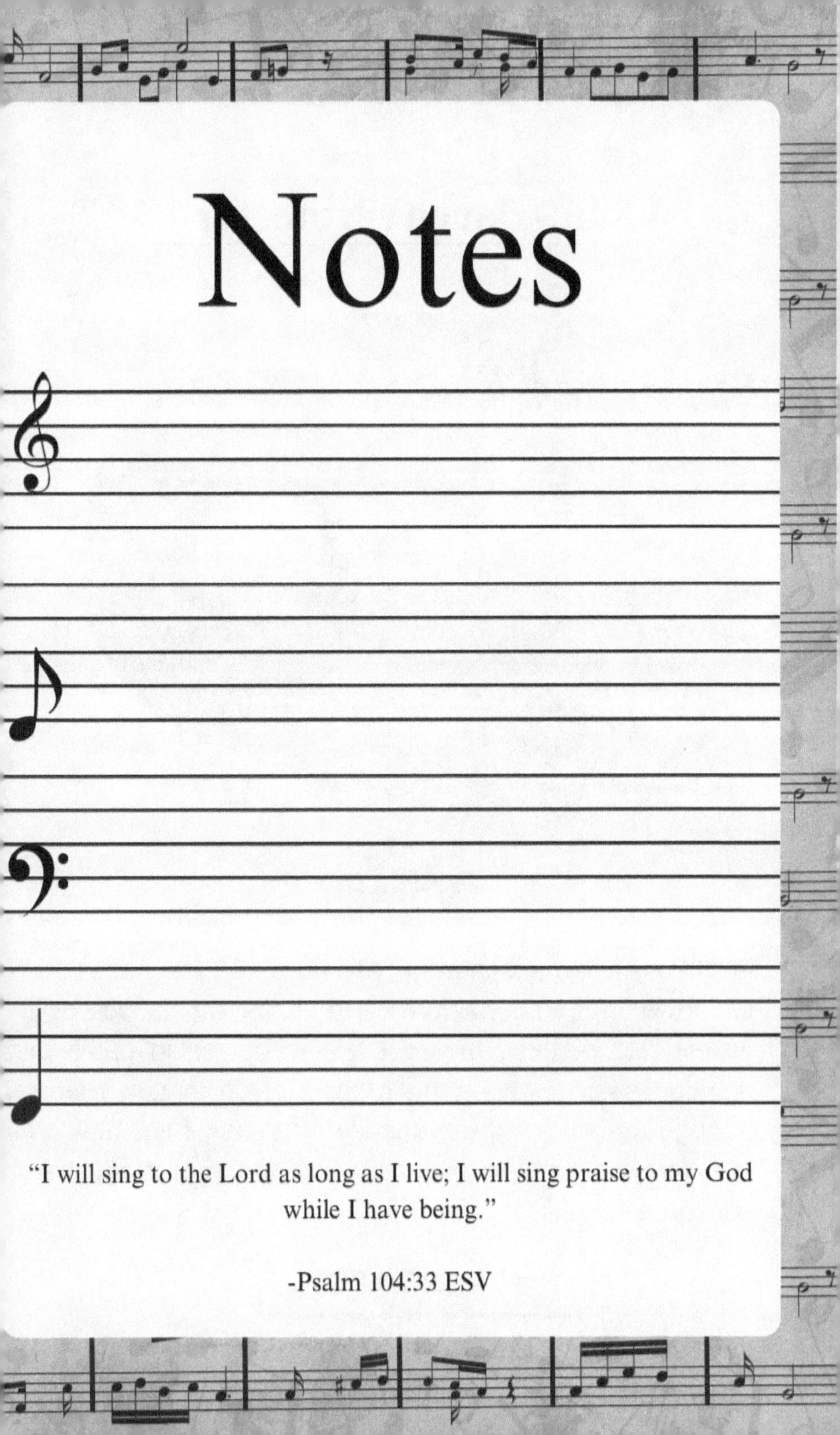

Notes

"I will sing to the Lord as long as I live; I will sing praise to my God while I have being."

-Psalm 104:33 ESV

A Safe-Haven (Protector)

Verses

"The Lord is my shepherd; I shall not want. He makes me lie down in green pastures. He leads me beside still waters. He restores my soul. He leads me in paths of righteousness for his name's sake. Even though I walk through the valley of the shadow of death, I will fear no evil, for you are with me; your rod and your staff, they comfort me."

Psalm 23:1-4 ESV

Your significant other has been abusing you for years, and today, you finally decide that enough is enough. They leave for work like any other night, but you've finally reached your breaking point. You choose to flee this time. Usually, you would clam up at the thought of leaving due to fear and intimidation. Truthfully, you've had several failed exit plans, some derailed by your significant other, but most derailed by imprisonment in your mind. But all caution is to the wind this time. You break for it while the coast is clear, taking only the clothes on your back, your wallet, and a few dollars in your left back pocket. Nothing else. It's pitch black outside, and you're terrified, but with time not on your side, you know, it's now or never. After all, they'll be home soon, and so, you figure, what's worse, being frightened for a moment and taking your life back, or being scared for a lifetime with no guarantee of making it out alive? Running down that long stretch of road, your heart is pounding, and you're gasping for air. You see headlights in the distance, so you briefly crouch down in a wooded area on the side of the road, out of view, until you see the headlights pass. Once they do, you resume running, keeping a watchful eye on your surroundings until you stumble upon a heavily populated area, and you take the opportunity to blend in with the crowd, ensuring you don't draw any unwanted attention to yourself. While in the crowd, you spot an alley off in the distance, and with your adrenaline still on high, you go for it. You have no plan per se, but you figure that going off the grid and getting as far away as possible will unlock the starting journey to your freedom, and little do you know, you are right.

Put yourself in this situation. Now, imagine the crippling feeling you would feel walking down that alley alone on a dark and cold night. Can you envision constantly looking over your shoulder in fear or hearing the sounds of stray animals rummaging in the night? How about the mental anguish of wondering whether or not your abuser will track and capture you? A mountain of doubt weighs on your shoulders, but you press on, knowing that just as God was with you in the physical beating and pressing you endured, keeping you alive when you were inches away from losing your life on several occasions. God is also with you when you are in your breakout. Finally, you make it to the end of that alley and face yet another decision. You are at a crossroads. You have no idea whether you should go left or right. But at that moment, you ask God, who tells you to go left. And because you are desperate to take your life back, you obey his voice. At this moment, God allows you to cross paths with a couple walking their dog. You look up to the sky, confused and gasping for air. *"God, you sent me this way for a man, a woman, and a dog?"* You thought to yourself, but before you could gripe[10],

---

[10] Gripe: to complain or nag

you suddenly felt a wave of peace overcome you. The husband spots you first, and immediately, his discernment goes into overdrive. "I don't want to alarm you, but the spirit tells me you need our help. Are you okay? Have you eaten? Do you need any assistance?" You stand there in silence. Fear flushed across your face. He looks affectionately at his wife and gives her a gentle nudge in that direction.

"Excuse me, God wanted you to cross paths with my husband and me. I hear it in my spirit. Do you need help? Don't be afraid. Always remember, "Be strong and courageous. Do not be afraid of anything, for the Lord your God goes with you; he will never leave or forsake you." (**Deuteronomy 31:6 NIV**) I don't know what you're going through, but know that God sent us here to help you. You don't have to say it aloud, but I hope you will acknowledge it. As the first step to your freedom is acknowledgment." She affectionately grabs your hand and continues, "Give me some sign, whatever you're most comfortable with. Squeeze my hand, nod your head, something to acknowledge that we are correct in our discernment. I need you to put it into the atmosphere so we know where to start." You let out a deep sigh and then squeezed her hand twice. Step one: check. You regained your power and finally acknowledged that you had a problem and needed help.

You may ask yourself, "How does this example relate to the scripture?" Being the victim of an abusive relationship, literally and figuratively, traps you in a valley that shadows death. To elaborate further, I wanted to start by briefly breaking down the definition of shadow. The term **Shadow** is a dark figure cast upon a surface by a body intercepting the rays from a light source. Tying that into the example, the dark figure in this instance represents your partner because they are diminishing your light by making you feel like you are unworthy of living a life free from control, manipulation, and bondage, and giving you the pretense that you have no way of life without them. As a result, the shadow of doubt is cast upon your mind, tricking you into believing they are right. In addition, depending on the level of the abuse you are experiencing, the shadow of death can also be consuming you in the sense that you can be one decision away from losing your life. One wrong move, one outward thought, one last word, one failed escape plan, and your end is in their hands. Talk about a terrifying type of power! In sum, the shadow of death can loom[11] over your head if you are not obedient in your escape. And your abuser is physically, mentally, and emotionally given the power to intercept[12] your being. All that you are becomes entangled in their web of deceit. And just like the enemy, their fulfillment comes in attacking your view of self and your relationship with the father, for they

---

[11] To loom is to linger or to appear in an exaggerated manner

[12] Intercept: to gain possession of / to stop, seize, or interrupt in progress or course or before arrival

know that a sense of community and self-worth can catapult you to a level they refuse for you to reach.

A secondary definition of shadow is an inseparable companion or follower. And just like most abusers, separation is often the driving force behind their control. Because typically, when you separate, you elevate, which removes them from that position of authority in your life. But just like the example above, when you take your power back and break free from bondage, and you're obedient, following the voice of God and moving whenever he tells you to, he will carry you in those valleys. You know? Those long seasons where everything seems stagnant. It's similar to being stuck in that alley while deciding whether to go left or right. But as soon as you took that step in the right direction, God sent a lifeline. And just as those strangers were there to rescue you in your time of need, God is the same. When you listen to the voice of God in your valley, and you remain courageous, he will not only give you a way out but also lead you toward green pastures and still waters. What does that mean, you ask? In short, the green pastures and still waters, in this instance, represent God leading you to safety and restoration.

God sometimes allows strangers to be in the right place, at the right time, to assist in removing you from harm's way. But removal isn't the sole benefit whenever God is on your side. In addition, it will lead you to overflow, causing you to go from lack to abundance, and fight or flight to freedom. Because, let's say, hypothetically speaking, that those strangers you met were the founders of a domestic abuse shelter. And say, they provided you a place to stay until you get on your feet, hot meals, and resources to gain employment. Setting you up to succeed. You would now have a place to rest; whether you're resting your mind, body, or soul, rest is essential when you've been in a constant fight or flight. It's important to realize that abusive relationships can figuratively drain the life out of you. If you've been there before, I'm sure you can relate to the relief you feel when you no longer have to run for your life and can rest assured that everything will be okay. You can live without looking over your shoulder, laugh without limits, and share your innermost thoughts without being silenced by someone who claims to 'love' you.

Lastly, you'd gain a peace that surpasses all understanding, allowing you to slowly but surely return to being YOU. The YOU that you used to be before the manipulation. But to receive it, you have to follow a few simple rules: one, ensuring that you remove those people, places, or things that are no longer serving you, even if you have to remove them forcefully. Deciding to run away is not only courageous but a bold and forced move that says, "I'm worthy, I'm taking my life back, and I deserve more than a life full of disappointment and despair. I deserve to be free."

Two, remembering to call on God in your darkest hour and to stop and listen carefully to his instructions. And three, being diligent about taking the lifelines that God gives you when he gives them to you. And not stalling. Don't deny his deliverance because it may not look as you thought. For instance, in that split second, hesitation regarding whether or not you should take assistance from the lovely couple is essential. Now I'm not saying you should throw your caution to the wind. Instead, it's to say that we often ignore the very people God sends to help us. So be careful not to delay your deliverance due to your discomfort. You never know who God assigns to your deliverance. Relinquish control and allow yourself to be set free. It can be the difference between your freedom and your finale. So think on your feet.

Now, maybe you can't relate to being in an abusive or controlling relationship. However, that doesn't mean this section doesn't apply to you, for everyone encounters valleys. With that said, what are those valleys in your life? Those dark places, situations where you feel stagnant? Those near-death situations you survived? What about those green pastures and still waters? Those places of comfort, feeding, hiding, safety, refreshment, and rest? What does that look like for you? Take a few moments to reflect.

Notes
"I will sing of your love and justice; to you, Lord, I will sing praise."
-Psalms 101:1 NIV

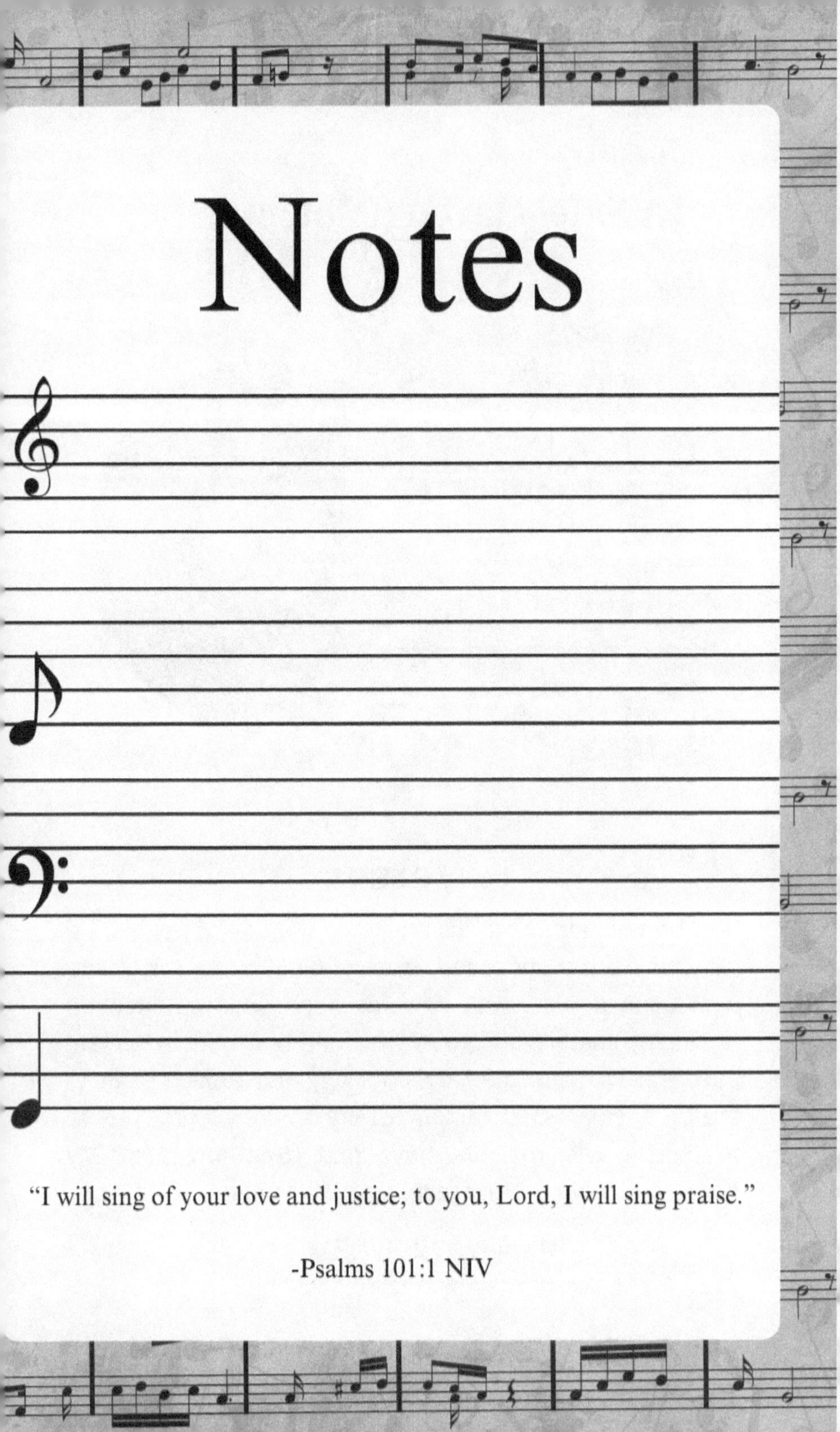

Notes

"I will sing of your love and justice; to you, Lord, I will sing praise."

-Psalms 101:1 NIV

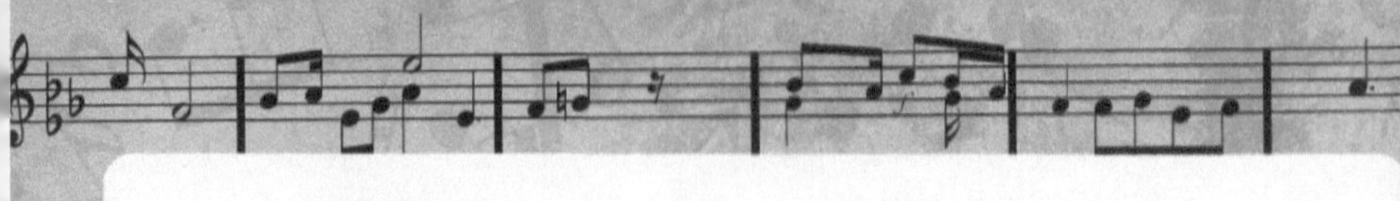

A Safe–Haven (Protector)

Verses

"For he will hide me in his shelter in the day of trouble; he will conceal me under the cover of his tent; he will lift me high upon a rock. And now my head shall be lifted up above my enemies all around me, and I will offer in his tent sacrifices with shouts of joy; I will sing and make melody to the Lord. Hear, O Lord, when I cry aloud; be gracious to me and answer me! You have said, "Seek my face." My heart says to you, "Your face, Lord, do I seek."

Psalm 27:5-8 ESV

*L*et's reflect on your inner child for a little bit. Now, imagine you're a kid again and at recess time. *Thud*! The sound your body makes as you impact the rubber mulch on the playground. The creak of the swing swaying back and forth over your head echoes in the background. You look up at the sky in anguish. Luckily, a friendly kid on the playground offers a helping hand to pull you up off the ground. You arise visibly shaken and feel embarrassment flow through your body. "Thank you," you say softly to the kind kid. You hear cackling and see people pointing at you from a distance. With a face full of tears, you take off running straight to your source of safety at school, Mrs. Snare, the school counselor's office.

How did I end up lying on the ground, you ask? Short answer: Aria, the school bully.

For years, and without reason, Aria has harassed and belittled you, and as long as she knows that she can do it, she continues to do it. After all, who's going to stop her? No parent-teacher conferences, revoking recess privileges, and switching classroom schedules would deter her from picking at you at any chance she got. Regardless of the preventative measures put in place, it's as if the more you asked for help, and the more you distanced yourself from her, the more she targeted you.

If you were anything like me as a kid, you could identify with me when I say I was the socially awkward, overly anxious, timid girl in life and school. While most people feel that being shy makes you go "under the radar" and takes you "out of the line of fire," sometimes being considered "different" often comes with unfair consequences. And more often than not, you are put on blast for things that are usually beyond your control. For instance, as in the above bullying example, sometimes staying out of the way or even being kind can still make you a target. The reality is that although we hear this all the time, we must realize that we are just like Jesus. In sum, we face trials because we are God's reflection. Jesus was perfect, yet he still suffered and was often ridiculed and mocked by people who didn't believe in him. We are no different. You become an automatic target to those out of alignment with God whenever he chooses you. But you must realize that it is not necessarily something you did that causes people to rise against you and attack; instead, it could simply be the anointing attached to you.

Although that seems unfair, it all boils down to the fact that when people can see the light in you that you can't see in yourself, they often want to dim it because they can't understand why YOU have it, and they don't. Or, they could have animosity towards you just because you have something materialistic that they don't possess. For instance, if you're a kid with the newest pair of shoes or a shiny new lunchbox, you may get chastised simply because the other kids around you don't have those things. Maybe they're jealous because they want to be the first to show off something new. You beat them to it, which angered them, or in most cases, they may realize that their parent can't afford to buy them nice things like yours can, so as a result, they'll do everything in their power to break you down just so that you feel bad for being blessed. However, you cannot let them win. You must understand that **what is for YOU is for you**. And you cannot apologize for what God and your parents choose to do in your life. In addition, you must realize that all these things that come against you are distractions that cause you to be out of alignment with God. The devil is a thief who "comes only to steal and kill and destroy" (See **John 10:10 ESV**), everything meant to propel you. And most times, the devil will assume the personalities of those around you, causing them to display characteristics such as anger, jealousy, insecurity, or a combination of several things at once to pull you off track.

With that said, Aria's decision to push you off the swings could have been fueled by one or several of those emotions. But the reality is, most children lack emotional training. And rightfully so, because if the adults around them have no emotional control, the children likely won't. Children often mirror what they see. So if they're not seeing proper displays of emotion at home, they won't exhibit those behaviors in society. So instead of smiling at you, they'll shove you. Or instead of complimenting your shoes, they'll step on them, scuff them, and laugh when you get offended by their actions because, to them, they've done nothing wrong. It oftentimes takes years of trial and error to get it right. The Bible says, "When I was a child, I talked like a child, I thought like a child, I reasoned like a child. When I became a man, I put the ways of childhood behind me." (**1 Corinthians 13:11 NIV**). That passage means we don't necessarily have a whole concept of right or wrong when we're children. But as we age, we discover different ways to manage our thoughts, feelings, and emotions. So, although Aria's actions are hurtful both in the moment and in your memory, you can't fault her entirely because she was a product of her environment. Sometimes you have to step back and let God do the correcting. And I don't know about you, but I know that no amount of human retaliation compares to God's wrath. So when you're in harm's way, remember him; he will keep you safe.

The beautiful thing about having God in your corner is that, although the trials may sting, God will always remain a refuge, a haven in your time of need. In other words, although the impact of the push hurt you not only mentally but physically, as a result of your embarrassment in front of all of the other kids at recess and then, when it was all over, you were still left with the residue, as you got up with visible scrapes and cuts on your body, serving as a visual reminder of the whole ordeal. But the beauty amid the ashes is that once you got up again, you could run to someone you trusted, who served as the calm in your storm. That person was Mrs. Snare, the school guidance counselor. Someone who quickly went from 'the nice lady who went out of her way to speak to you every morning,' to a warm, maternal-like figure in your life. She would do check-ins daily, ensuring you felt safe, supported, and confident. And just as Mrs. Snare served as your safety net at school by nursing your wounds, calming you down, allowing you to finish the rest of your school day in her office, and keeping a watchful and supportive eye on you throughout the entire school year, God does the same for us. So anytime you feel unsafe, remember that God is only one call away—not a physical call via a telephone, of course, but a voice call. Dial into him and seek his face whenever you feel unsafe, and he will provide you with safety in his dwelling place.

Notes
"Sing the glory of his name; make his praise glorious."
-Psalms 66:2 NIV

Notes

"Sing the glory of his name; make his praise glorious."

-Psalms 66:2 NIV

A Safe-Haven (Protector)

Verse

"No weapon that is formed against thee shall prosper; and every tongue that shall rise against thee in judgment thou shalt condemn. This is the heritage of the servants of Jehovah, and their righteousness which is of me, saith Jehovah."

Isaiah 54:17 ASV

After twenty-two years of marriage, your husband drops a bombshell and says those four words no woman madly in love with her spouse ever wants to hear: "I want a divorce." You are baffled because, before his announcement, you envisioned your marriage as the picture of perfection. Your husband was attentive to you and the children, reciprocal in household duties, dedicated, caring, respectful, and chivalrous: holding doors for you, laying down his jacket so your shoes don't get wet, opening your car door—all of the things that don't scream there's a shift in the foundation of your relationship. You and he openly communicate with one another, partake in routine date nights, have lots of fun together, and put each other first at all costs, so hearing those words out of his mouth leaves you blindsided. *"Is it something I did? Is it something I said? I don't understand!"* You ask yourself. But all he says is, "It's not you; it's me. I think you're perfect; I want to experience life outside marriage. I'm just trying to see if it's worth it. I've been married longer than I've been single and am at a crossroads." A golf ball-sized lump forms in your throat. And you can't stop the tears from falling. As bad as you tried to resist and fight, you know that he stands firm when he makes up his mind. So, to your disdain, you oblige and give him what he wants.

A million thoughts run through your head. You often sacrifice much of yourself as a spouse to appease your partner's needs. Losing all of who you are and assuming everything that he wanted, needed, and desired you to be. You put your dreams on hold so that he could prioritize his dreams. You gave him children and reared them to the best of your abilities. You kept a tidy home, cooked hot meals daily, and catered to his needs as much as he catered to yours. And now, you can't help but wonder, *"Was it all for nothing?"*

One day, instead of wallowing in your pity, you force yourself out of bed and head to complete a much-needed grocery run. Although you are still navigating how to maneuver through the remnants of what once was your union, you know you can't sit on the sidelines of your life. You must continue to show up even when you feel like you can't. The pain still lingers, yet you push forward as best you can. While exiting the checkout line, you encounter a mutual "friend" between you and your ex-husband. "Girl, I'm surprised you know how to maneuver without-" she says condescendingly. Before she can say his name, you cut her short. "I was someone before him, and I'll be someone without him. But I hope you have a blessed day." And you brush past her, purposely bumping shoulders. Upon passing, she murmurs, "That's why you couldn't keep him. With an attitude like that, who would want YOU!" She rolls her eyes and smirks. Just as you are about to snap, a little old lady heads towards you and firmly grasps your hand.

"Sweetheart, I know we don't know one another, and I don't know your situation, but I just want to say it's not worth it. Whatever the issue is between you, don't let it get the best of you." You take a deep breath, inhale, and immediately exhale. You're still fuming inside, but you know the lady is correct. "Walk with me," she says. You both walk out of the store, and she pulls you to the side, away from the incoming store traffic. "Do you mind if I pray for you?" Once she finished, you let out a sigh of relief. "Thank you so much, ma'am. God bless you." You embrace her and head towards your car, feeling much better and level-headed afterward. The lesson in this example is that no matter how hard she tried to pierce you in your side and slander your character in that supermarket, God sent an angel on earth to intervene and soothe the sting's impact right away.

On the contrary, say you're at a Friday night high school football game with friends. You notice a fight between two classmates and immediately spring into action to break it up. You manage to pull them apart and diffuse the situation; however, the feud is far from over. Once the game is over and everyone is walking back to their car, you notice one of your classmates involved in the altercation frantically fumbling around in their car. Your stomach feels like it drops to your feet, and your discernment tells you something isn't right. You say to your friends, "Let's go, y'all! I feel like something is about to happen." But they are too busy having fun and celebrating your school's big win, so they ignore you. You don't want to leave them, but you decide to cut through the crowd and make a beeline for your car to get a head start. Just as you close the driver-side door, shots ring out! "Pop! Pop! Pop," the sound of muffled screams and a herd of feet hitting the pavement at top speed echoes through your vehicle. You escape the parking lot and, coincidentally, drive up to your friends.

Everyone hops in the car, seemingly unharmed. You hurriedly drive off and breathe a sigh of relief —briefly. Heavy panting fills the car, drowning out the sound of the radio. Everyone's adrenaline is on high. "Ahhh!" your best friend, Key, loudly screams. You panic inside, but can't react like you want to since you are behind the wheel. "Omg! Key got hit!" your friend exclaims from the back seat. You start sweating profusely and head straight to the hospital nearby. Once there, you all flag down some help, and they immediately wheel her in. While waiting for the update, you dreadfully called Key's parents to explain everything. Luckily, they are not far away and arrive in no time. Running straight to the desk and then being whisked away into the back. After about thirty minutes, the doctor emerges and fills you all in. "She is not severely injured, thank God. This wound is only a minor abrasion. The bullet grazed her abdomen, and the sting from the wound was causing her some discomfort. But she's all disinfected and patched up and ready to go. Great job, friends. Quick thinking. It's always better to be safe than sorry, but she should heal normally in a week or so. And she will be discharged soon." Although the doctor's news relieves you, the situation still weighs heavily on your heart. You worry that her parents will blame you, even though she decided to stay behind despite your advice. You're grateful that your prayers worked, but the what-ifs consume you. So much so that while your friends try to get your attention, you've thoroughly checked out. After a few minutes of deep thought, you come to. Your other friend, Major, looks at you, places his hand on your shoulder, and says, "Don't blame yourself. You told us to come on, but we didn't listen. You did your part. Key and the rest of us learned a valuable lesson tonight. Listen to the warnings. Don't beat yourself up. Let's go home and get some rest. We'll check on Key in the morning."

The important lesson here, yet again, is that the weapon formed (i.e., Key did get grazed by a bullet), but it did not prosper (i.e., she did not lose her life, and she also was not severely injured). However, as Major said, sometimes catastrophic situations arise to teach us the simplest lessons, such as you can't ignore prophetic warnings and always follow your gut. That "gut feeling" is God giving you specific instructions. Two, this tells you that, despite who the direction is coming from, you never know what God is protecting you from. So take heed. For instance, many people ignore their friends and have a "you can't tell me what to do" attitude when they try to warn them of danger.

However, you must be careful to have that attitude toward caring and anointed people because they can protect you from things you can't see. And when you're disobedient, God can and will use extreme measures to get your attention, such as a near-death experience. But the beauty in this painful situation is that you can use this story to proclaim the dangers of not listening to instructions and the joy of coming out bruised but still unscathed.[13] So remember, as you go through the trials of life, that God never said weapons wouldn't form because they will. However, they can't pierce you with God as your defender.

---

[13] Unscathed, in this instance, is coming out "in one piece."

Notes

"Sing to him a new song; play skillfully, and shout for joy."

-Psalms 33:3 NIV

Notes

"Sing to him a new song; play skillfully, and shout for joy."

-Psalms 33:3 NIV

A Safe-Haven (Protector)

Verse

"Through you we push back our enemies; through your name we trample our foes. I put no trust in my bow, my sword does not bring me victory; but you give us victory over our enemies, you put our adversaries to shame. In God we make our boast all day long, and we will praise your name forever."

Psalms 44:5-8 NIV

You spend day and night preparing for your first boxing match. Countless hours of strength training, hand and eye coordination tactics, and conditioning drills. Besides some regular pre-match trash-talk, things seem to go smoothly leading up to the fight between you and your opponent. You are in your zone, totally focused, eating clean, not partaking in extracurricular activities such as drinking or smoking, abstaining from marital relations with your wife, and getting adequate sleep. You are not allowing any distractions to throw you off your pivot. You are highly disciplined and determined to win. The organization requests an initial drug test a few weeks before the boxing match. After a few days, your results return, and you are clear to compete; the test returns negative for all substances. You continue with your routine and training up until the big day. Finally, the day arrives, and you are experiencing a mixture of emotions. You are hyped up and excited to have your first professional fight, but there's still a slight nervous flutter in your gut.

"Shake it off, Canon, you got this!" You walk into the double doors of the arena, and as soon as you arrive, they escort you to your dressing room to begin your preparation process. After a brief huddle and a prayer, you emerge from the dressing

room ready to fight. The announcer calls your name, and you sprint out from the back, bob and weave between the ropes, and enter the ring. Your opponent also enters the ring and is introduced. After amicably bumping gloves and a "LET'S GET READYYY TO RUMBLLLEEE!" from the announcer, the fight begins. You start strong, ducking and weaving his jabs.

You land the first punch to his face. The impact causes him to stumble. While he's off guard, you get a few more licks in and one final right hook that knocks your opponent on his back. After a few seconds lying flat, he gets back up. Again, he tries to land a punch but misses. The victory is in your favor at this point. But then, things took a turn. After a brief rest period, the match resumes. In the second round, you land three punches. You draw your arm back in preparation for the fourth punch. Your opponent forcefully headbutts[14] you in the gut and knocks you to your knees. You look to the referee, hoping for a disqualification for the deliberate act; however, he only gets a warning. You arise both focused and frustrated. *Swoosh!* You land the uppercut that draws blood from the lip of your opponent, followed by three more jabs. The final jab knocks your opponent out for the

---

[14] Head-butting is illegal in the sport of boxing and most times results in disqualification.

second time. You hoped for a TKO (technical knock out), but he got up with one second to spare.

Now in round four, he comes in strong, landing two jabs, but when he tries to land a third, you dodge the punch and hit him with a hard right hook, causing him to stumble. He takes a deep breath in, visibly frustrated. He swings and comes up void. You then regain control. Just as you're about to land a right hook, he hits you with several low blows[15]: one to your gut, and two to your nether regions, causing his disqualification by unanimous decision.

This boxing example shows that God sometimes allows us to fight in the ring with the enemy. And doing so, we may get knocked off our pivot, laid out on our back, battered or bruised, but in the end, he will swoop in and claim the victory for us without us even having to finish the fight. For instance, a full boxing match lasts roughly twelve rounds. However, when God is on your side, he will allow you to finish prematurely. Recall how, in the example, Canon won by unanimous decision, in only four short rounds. He didn't even have to go all twelve rounds and still came out with the victory. That is the beauty of having a God-centered life. But remember, the enemy will

---

[15] Low blows are punches to the lower abdomen or groin area; these are also illegal in the sport. If done repeatedly, they can result in disqualification.

not go down easily in this head-to-head. The devil will do anything to knock you off your feet, even if that means fighting dirty.

In the same way, Canon's opponent used several illegal tactics, such as low blows and headbutting, to sway the fight; the enemy will do the same to sway you in life. He'll make you think that God isn't there, your friends or family members don't care, you'll never win, etc. Imagine being cornered in the ring where your back is against the ropes, in full despair, with nowhere to turn and no way out. How about being drained of your energy and never being replenished? But the beauty in a Christ-centered life is that when you think it's over for you and think to yourself, *"everyone else is cheating their way through it except me,"* God steps in. When you think no one will advocate for you, God steps in. Not only does he step in, he also steps into the ring with intention, just like the referee, and declares you the victor unanimously. Now take a few moments to reflect. Was there a situation or three where life had you backed against the ropes? Did you see no means of escape, yet God still brought you out and declared you victorious?

Notes

"All the earth bows down to you; they sing praise to you,
they sing the praises of your name."

-Psalms 66:4 NIV

Notes

"All the earth bows down to you; they sing praise to you,
they sing the praises of your name."

-Psalms 66:4 NIV

A Good Listener

Verse

"I love the Lord, for he heard my voice; he heard my cry for mercy. Because he turned his ear to me, I will call on him as long as I live. The cords of death entangled me, the anguish of the grave came over me; I was overcome by distress and sorrow. Then I called on the name of the Lord: "Lord, save me!" The Lord is gracious and righteous; our God is full of compassion. The Lord protects the unwary; when I was brought low, he saved me. Return to your rest, my soul, for the Lord has been good to you."

Psalms 116:1-7 NIV

You are in the first trimester of your pregnancy, and you and your husband are so excited. Both of you had been praying and fasting for over seven years to conceive a child, and finally, God answered your prayers. Late one night, you are jolted awake, and a stabbing pain shoots through your abdomen. "Ouch! Ouch," you wince in pain. Curling yourself into a fetal position on the bed. Your husband is startled awake by your groans. "Baby, are you okay?" he exclaims. But you can't get the words out. The pain figuratively knocks the wind out of you. Your husband, although still groggy, jumps into action. Turning on the overhead light on his side of the bed to illuminate the room, and then coming over to your side of the bed to try to console you, when suddenly, blood begins rushing down your leg. He picks up the phone and immediately dials 911. No questions asked. Calmly, he explains, "Hello Operator, I believe my wife may be suffering a miscarriage. Please send help as quickly as you can." Hearing him say the term miscarriage was yet another punch to the gut. The tears begin flowing down your face. "It's okay, baby! It's okay. I got you! Help is on the way!" His voice is the calm amid your hysteria. While you wait for the ambulance, your husband packs a hospital bag and sets it by the front door, and then he comes back up the stairs, quickly cleans you up to the best of his abilities, wraps you up in the top sheet, and carefully picks you up off the bed. Just as he's carrying you down the stairs, there's a knock at the door. It's the Paramedics.

The ride to the hospital, although quick, is silent and somber. But your husband is there every step of the way. And because you have lost a significant amount of blood, you have been whisked away to a hospital room swiftly and immediately. Once the doctor arrives and conducts an ultrasound, she confirms. You miscarried. "Mrs. Zamir, you suffered an incomplete miscarriage. Which means that when you were startled awake and bleeding profusely, you did pass some of the tissue from the pregnancy; however, you did not pass all of it. I would say wait and allow the remaining tissue to pass independently with most patients. However, because you have lost such a significant amount of blood, we are going to have to perform a D&C or a dilation and curettage to expel the remaining tissue from your body, because if we leave it, it can cause you to have prolonged bleeding or, in the worst case scenario, hemorrhage or infection."

As much as you want to cry a river, you cried so much leading up to the hospital visit that you're in a state of numbness. You can't cry, talk, or think. You stare blankly at the whiteboard, obsessing over what's written. The time is 2:22am. Dr. Canto is the doctor. And your nurse's name is Harmony. *How ironic*, you thought. Since everything in your life seems out of tune, Dr. Canto continues, "the D&C should only take about 10-15 minutes to complete. But you must stay until about 8:00am, so we can monitor you for a few hours before releasing you. I will step out for a few minutes and prep for the procedure. The nurse will administer your anesthesia shortly, and then you'll be wheeled into the OR (Operating Room)." When she leaves, you cry out to God for mercy. "Why, God, why? My baby. Our baby is gone. Lord, please have mercy on me in this moment. Because I do trust that you said we'd be parents this year, but to say I'm not hurting right now would be a lie. Lord, you know how much we want to be parents." After a deep breath and a quick wipe of the eyes, you do your best to 'suck it up!' And you do so just in time, as the nurse reenters the hospital room and administers your anesthesia. You do your best to appear strong, but she looks in your eyes, and you have a silent understanding. "I know it doesn't feel good right now, but you will see glory in the end," she says. You're still speechless, but you nod in agreement and give her a gentle squeeze on the hand. *She has no idea how much I needed that*, you thought to yourself. You're wide awake, they wheel you away, but by the time you go into surgery, you've drifted off into a deep sleep. The procedure is over when you wake up, and the doctor hovers over you.

 "Mrs. Zamir! Mrs. Zamir! Can you hear me? The procedure was a success." Your Nurse Harmony will escort you back to your room to recover for a few hours. And once you're in the clear, you will be discharged." Once discharged, your husband cautiously escorts you to the car. When you arrive home, he walks you into the living room and places you on the chaise at the end of your sectional, allowing you to stretch out comfortably and rest. He ensures you have blankets, snacks, the whole nine at your disposal. Once he gets you situated, he kisses you on the cheek and heads upstairs to clean. Before he could get to the second step, you exclaim. "I'm sorry, babe. I'm so sorry I couldn't give you a child." He immediately makes a beeline, sits on the edge of the chaise, and places his hand on your face. "No. Don't you dare. I love you and I'm here for you and WITH you. And I don't blame you. I say it's not our time yet. But in due time, we will be the parents of a healthy baby. Get some rest, baby, it's going to be okay. " He sits there, holding you in his arms until you fall asleep. You have cried yourself into exhaustion.

Once you are sound asleep, he heads upstairs. The first step is to spot treat the mattress and allow it to dry while throwing the soiled bedding and the nightgown you wore to the hospital into the washing machine. Once that's complete, he heads back downstairs to check in, and you're still down for the count. Suddenly, there's a knock at the door. It's your mom. Of course, your husband texted your parents every step of the way and kept them in the loop, both when you left and upon your return home. She glances at the chaise and sees you still asleep, so she softly kisses you on the cheek, careful not to disturb you, and immediately offers a helping hand around the house, ensuring that you don't have to lift a finger when you wake.

Fast forward a few months, and while you're still dealing, you're also healing. You and your husband have been attending grief counseling with your pastor, and he has been praying over your life, health, and your womb at the end of each session. You are more at ease, but still a bit uneasy. Cautious, yet confident. But you relax and let it happen as the pastor keeps reiterating. So much so that exactly seven months to the date of your D&C, you went in for a routine check-up and found out you were pregnant again. It is a pleasant surprise to you and your husband, as you didn't notice anything unusual with your body. You just equated minimal weight gain to "happy weight" and maybe a new obsession with French fries, to "girl cravings," but nothing that alarmed you. And this time, the doctor has great news. You have not only made it past the danger zone, as you were further along in the pregnancy than anticipated, twenty weeks to be exact, but you also find out you are carrying twins. Yes, twins!

After a brief examination, the doctor mentions that you have a retroverted or tilted uterus, causing the babies to grow inward and not outward for the first few months, which would explain why you weren't showing. However, she said that nothing appeared abnormal outside of that, the babies seemed very healthy, and you should notice your stomach begin to grow outward as normal in no time. "I will closely monitor you for the duration of this pregnancy just because of the prior miscarriage and the tilt in your uterus. But I am pleased to announce that all is well thus far." You squeal in excitement. Nervous that time is slipping away, but excited for the blessings God is bestowing upon you and your significant other.

And in what seemed like the blink of an eye, you and your husband finally brought home two healthy, happy, and full-term babies. A boy and a girl whom you affectionately name Ronen (Hebrew for "Song or Joy" / One who sings or rejoices) and Raelin (English for "Beam of light" / Hebrew for Beauty/Song of the Gods). Carefully crafted names encapsulating how you and your husband feel in this full-circle moment. You are rejoicing in God's double portion, and your new twins are a beautiful reflection of God's love and a beam of light in the darkness that once consumed you. And while you still grieve over what was, you embrace the fullness of what is.

The beauty of this example is that we often feel as if God is not right there amid our devastation. But the thing about having a solid relationship with Christ is that he never leaves your side, even when it may feel as though he is absent. And it's important to note that every trial we endure never makes sense at the moment, but it is always for a greater purpose. For instance, without the loss of your first child, you wouldn't appreciate the birth of your twins as much as you do. You guard them with your lives because you realize how precious life is through loss. You shower them with love and affection because you know the void of being unable to love the child you lost. And you now have compassion for other women you never had before. From those with fertility and/or hormonal issues, to those without. You are careful not to police another woman's body, questioning when she's going to have children, because you now know for yourself that having children doesn't come easily to every woman, all bodies are not created equal, and all journeys are not the same. In other words, the loss brought forth a lesson in trusting God amid unfavorable situations, allowing yourself the space and the grace to grieve and still believe, and ultimately, a lesson in wholeheartedly loving without judgments or limits.

Most importantly, in addition to God never leaving your side, please remember that he hears every word you say and values your concerns. And as long as he knows you have a sincere heart posture when you come to him, he will pity your every groan, cry, gripe, and complaint. For instance, when she was crying out to God in the hospital bed, wondering why God had forsaken her family and taken away the child that they had been trying so hard to conceive, God heard every word, and he felt for her in that moment. So much so that he sent in reinforcements, people she was most comfortable with (i.e., her husband telling her that they would conceive in due time, her pastor praying over her womb, and Nurse Harmony's advice) to foreshadow what would come. That's another perk of being close to God. He will give you hints and show you glimpses of the bigger picture. However, it is up to us to hold on to the hints and keep the hope. Because the catch is, he doesn't tell us the process we'll have to endure to get there. And rightfully so, because if he told us the process to attain the things we genuinely want, none of us would have any of the blessings we possess. Why, you ask? Most don't want to endure the pressure to get to the promise. Using the example above, imagine how happy the Zamir's were after seven years of trying to conceive and becoming pregnant. But then, think of how she cried out to God in the loss as if the same God who implanted the baby can't be the same God to take the baby. And in the same breath, the same God who removed the baby from your womb can be the same God to restore your womb and multiply it. The word says, "Peace I leave with you; my peace I give you. I do not give to you as the world gives. Do not let your hearts be troubled and do not be afraid." (**John 14:27 NIV**). So, whether God gives or takes from your womb, you cannot trouble your heart. Feel the grief, yes, but amplify the trust that everything will work together for those who believe.

In sum, although parental grief is never easy, in this instance, you must realize that God often removes things from our lives and replaces them with something better. And by no means is that said in a way that reduces the life that you lost. Instead, it's to say that God will always give you "double for your trouble," in this case, getting double the babies is double the opportunity to love another version of yourself, and what's not beautiful about that?

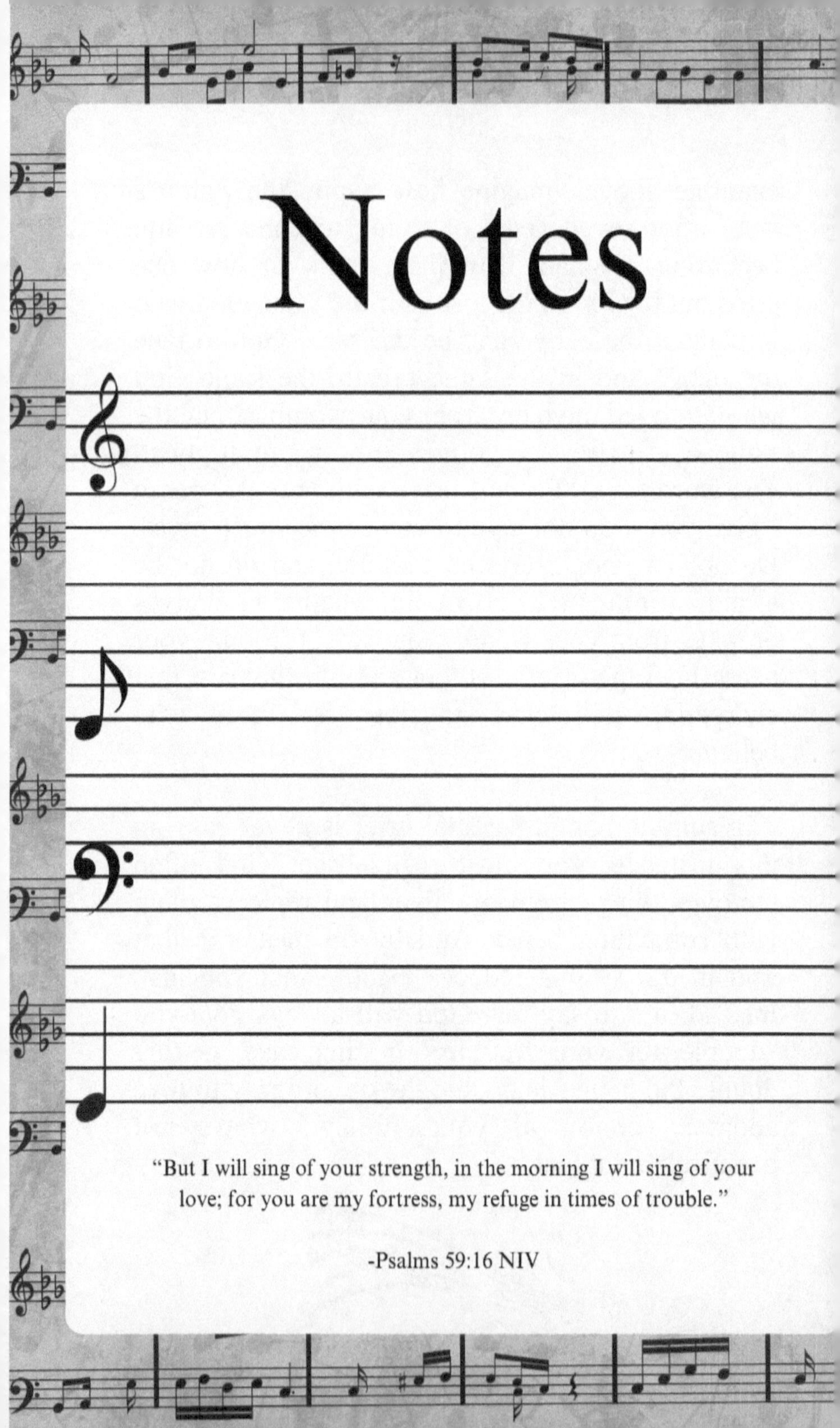

Notes

"But I will sing of your strength, in the morning I will sing of your love; for you are my fortress, my refuge in times of trouble."

-Psalms 59:16 NIV

Notes

"But I will sing of your strength, in the morning I will sing of your love; for you are my fortress, my refuge in times of trouble."

-Psalms 59:16 NIV

A Good Listener (Deliverer)

Verse

"Hear me, my God, as I voice my complaint; protect my life from the threat of the enemy. Hide me from the conspiracy of the wicked, from the plots of evildoers. They sharpen their tongues like swords and aim cruel words like deadly arrows. They shoot from ambush at the innocent; they shoot suddenly, without fear. They encourage each other in evil plans, they talk about hiding their snares; they say, "Who will see it?" They plot injustice and say, "We have devised a perfect plan!" Surely the human mind and heart are cunning. But God will shoot them with his arrows; they will suddenly be struck down. He will turn their own tongues against them and bring them to ruin; all who see them will shake their heads in scorn. All people will fear; they will proclaim the works of God and ponder what he has done. The righteous will rejoice in the Lord and take refuge in him; all the upright in heart will glory in him!"

Psalms 64:1-10 NIV

icture this: you're hanging out with your childhood best friend for the first time in a few years. She went off to college, out of state, and you decided to stay local for college, so although you both kept the lines of communication open daily through social media and FaceTime, you haven't seen each other in person in a while. She came home several times during college breaks, but time never permitted the two of you to get together. However, now that you have both graduated and she's home for good since landing her new role in town, you're excited that you have finally found some time to catch up that works best for both of you. You'll meet at a local sports bar / popular hangout spot that you'll use to frequent in high school for food and fellowship. It's just you and her like old times, and all was well. The conversation was great, y'all didn't miss a moment. There was no awkwardness, tension, or anything— just genuine love and support. The vibes in the sports bar were good, too. Everyone from the patrons to the servers was super friendly, the food was A1, just like you remembered, and the music didn't miss a beat. Y'all had so much fun catching up that, before she leaves, she asks you if you want to go to a local party with her tomorrow night. You're hesitant because you're not the party type, never have been. See you, you're more of the straight and narrow girl. You know, the one who tries her best to be her best. Most would call you a "perfectionist" or a "goody two-shoes," but you don't see it that way. Instead, you equate it to wanting to ensure that your every move is calculated and executed with as much purpose and intention as possible.

You understand the importance of having fun and enjoying your life, but you never felt like you had to drink, smoke, or party to enjoy your life. However, you noticed she had begun hanging around a coed group of wild partiers since college. But her energy remained the same when it came to you, so you continued being friends with her and equated it to 'different strokes for different folks.' In other words, while most best friends typically have much in common, they're still different people with different ideals who choose to love one another through it all. And staying friends with her, although you're in two different places, is a common compromise in friendships. So you didn't think you were doing anything out of the ordinary. *The closest of friends are often opposite. Just because she's having fun doesn't make her a bad person. Instead of judging her, I'll say a silent prayer for her.* You thought.

God, I pray that whatever peace she needs in her life, that may be causing her to hide behind these extreme behaviors, will be provided to her by you and only you, God. I ask that you remove whoever is not serving her in this season of her life. In your name, I pray, Amen.

You snap back to reality, prepared to make up an excuse about why you can't attend the party, but your mom calls and saves the day. You motioned your friend to pause while holding up one finger and diverting attention to the phone. "This is my mom. I have to take this. One second, girl." She nods in agreement. "I know you're hanging out today, but don't forget we're having family game night tomorrow night. Can you make the Rotel Dip, the Seafood Salad, and the Sliders for us? Also, can we have it at your house instead? I'll still be the host, but you have more space." You usually fret[16] about last-minute requests, but this time, you happily obliged.[17] "Yes, Ma! That's fine. And, yes, I got you! I'll go to the store as soon as I leave here. We're wrapping up in a few." Your friend yells from across the table, "Hey, Ma!" And before you could say anything else, your mom overhears her and says, "Tell my second daughter I said hello and to come to game night tomorrow, if she's not busy." You pause briefly. Then, continue. "I will. I love you. And I'll see you in a few." You end the call with your mom and relay the message to your bestie. "I forgot I have to cook and prep for game

---

[16] Fret: to constantly be worried or anxious (in this instance, to be uncomfortable)

Obliged: to do as someone asks to help or please them.

night tomorrow. My mom has been trying to put this night together for so long, especially since our family barely gets together anymore. I'll have to pass on the party; however, if you're up for it, swing through our game night for a bit before you head to your party. My momma said she wants to see you anyway. It'll be at my house. I'll text you the details and the address." She rises from the table and walks toward you, all thirty-two teeth showing, and arms extended. You both embrace. The hug is so sincere. "You know I'll be there, girl. I love y'all." She kisses you on the cheek. "And we love you back!" you said with a smile.

Fast-forward to game night, and you and your mom are wrapping up preparing everything for family and friends to arrive. Everyone, including your best friend, is texting and calling to let you know they're on the way. She asks if bringing a male friend is okay, and you don't see an issue. "Yeah, girl, that's fine. The more, the merrier." From the moment people started arriving, the vibes were immaculate. Everyone meshed, laughed nonstop, ate, participated in all the games, and talked trash all night. And bestie and her beau[18] fit right in. They stayed well into the night/morning, then left to head to the party, which was perfect for them because most parties like that don't crank up

---

[18] In this instance, Beau refers to a boyfriend / male admirer/friend of the opposite sex.

until the wee hours of the morning anyway. Before they left, you saw them both out to the car and thanked them for coming. "No, thank you, bestie, for inviting us. We had a blast. I'll check in with you tomorrow. I love you." After a brief embrace, an "I love you more!" between you and your bestie, and a quick and polite farewell from her Beau, you head back inside the house.

Almost everyone spent the night since you stayed up all night long. The next morning, one of your cousins was nice enough to clean the house and prepare breakfast for everyone. After breakfast, everyone freshened up and phased out, leaving you and your mom with much-needed mommy-daughter time. You both lay around for a while, but ultimately, you headed to the mall for some retail therapy, followed by the nail shop for a mani and pedi, and the spa for a massage. You rise from the massage table refreshed and ready to head home and relax. Your mom asks if she could stay another night, and y'all watch movies and chill. "Sure, Mommy! I'd love that!" The ride home was peaceful, almost too calm. But when you pulled into your driveway, that peace quickly turned to pain. "Omg! You've got to be kidding me right now!" The tears are rolling, and your heart is beating perfusely. You slowly exit the car, your mom standing by your side, and while standing in the yard, you dial 911. "Hello operator, my home has been vandalized." Although it felt like an hour, only a few short minutes later, the police arrived. Upon exiting the police cruiser, one of the officers approaches you and wants to ensure that neither you nor your mother entered the premises before their arrival.

"No, sir, we have not! We just got here. When I pulled in the driveway, I noticed the door was ajar, but I knew I had locked it before we left." A glimmer of hope fills your heart as you realize that in the heat of the moment, your cameras were not damaged or disconnected during the home invasion. You equate that to your security company's excellent blending skills. You know exactly where to look for the red dot from the master camera, and your eye spots it immediately. "I noticed the perpetrators didn't disconnect the cameras during the home invasion. The master camera light is still on. So, prayfully, the footage can bring us some insight."

Once the police determined the coast was clear inside the house, you escorted them to your locked security room and rolled back the footage from today. They saw everything clearly, inside and out: your cousin cooking breakfast, family members leaving one by one, you and your mom lying around, and then heading out for the day. As you suspected, the camera caught you double-checking that you locked the door and the windows before pulling off. In addition, security footage captures a car pulling into your yard roughly an hour after you leave. "Do you recognize this car?" one of the officers asks, but neither of you does. *Who else could know where I stay?* You thought. *I wouldn't invite anyone I don't know or trust into my home.* Suddenly, the two assailants emerge from the vehicle. The driver you've never seen before. But the passenger, you recognize right away. "Ma, that's the guy from last night. The one who showed up with sis![19] I know that's him. I remember that tattoo on his arm!"

The cop zooms in on the tattoo on his arm and takes screenclips. They gather screen clippings of their faces, the vehicle, the license plate, and other relevant details, and file a police report. Before they leave, they do an escorted walk-through with you. Luckily, you have pictures of everything in your home, so you can easily recall if anything is missing. And to your surprise. Nothing is out of place, and everything is intact. Ironically, your phone rings and it's your "bestie." But you find it sketchy that she calls as soon as you identify her Beau as one of the perpetrators, so you don't answer. She calls again, same thing. As the police exit the premises, your elderly neighbor walks

---

[19] "Sis" was a term of endearment you used for your bestie because you viewed her as a sister.

outside and offers additional insight and evidence to the police. "I'm sorry that happened to you, and I wanted to intervene even more. Truly, I did. But I'm old, and I didn't want anyone to hurt me. I did say, Who are you? And what are you guys doing here? Over the loudspeaker. And I believe they may have gotten scared and fled at the sound of my voice." You pause to process it all. "Thank you, you've done more than enough, sir." Your neighbor asks if you need anything, and you shake your head. "No, I'm okay. Thanks again for all of your help." He smiles at you and heads back inside, and the police head back to the station.

While still outside, you call your insurance company to report the incident. Luckily, your mom has a connection at a glass/window company, and she steps inside the house simultaneously to schedule an emergency appointment. "We have one same-day appointment left." *Look at God!* She thought. Hours later, your window is as good as new. But in the meantime, you borrow your mom's phone while yours is on the charger to return a call to your cousin, who also called amid the chaos, and fill her in on what occurred. Y'all sit outside on the porch and chat with her to pass the time.

You can hear your phone ringing repeatedly from inside the house, but you already know who it is, and you refuse to answer it, so angry that you act impulsively. And good thing you didn't, because your cousin sent a voicenote to the group chat between you, her, and your mom, that flipped everything you thought you knew upside down. Your "bestie" admitted to having her new Beau and his friend set you up /attempt to steal from you. But they didn't anticipate your neighbor being home and derailing their plans. Long story short, she got into it with one of her old friends from college, and in retaliation, the ex-friend leaked the audio clips: "I never liked her anyway. She always thought she was better than everybody, and I wanted her to hurt like I was hurting. I hope they stick her up for everything she has." Those words echoed in your head over and over again. *Wow!* You thought. *To think that low of me that you potentially put my life in danger and then call me repeatedly as if you did nothing wrong. The nerve of you! Some "bestie" you are to me.* You reflect on the betrayal.

Bestie calls again, this time leaving a voicemail that appears sincere. "Hey, bestie, just checking in on you. Thank you for inviting us last night. I had such a good time. Call me when you get a chance. I love you forever!" But instead of going back and forth, trying to prove a point, you send a copy of the voicenote with the following message: "I love you as Christ loves us, and I forgive you. I don't wish you any ill will or despise you for what you did. But I want to give you the distance you desire from me."

Final step, 'block caller.'

I remember my dad used to tell me as a kid, **"One who wants friends, must first show himself friendly"** (see **Proverbs 18:24 NIV**), and that is a saying that I've lived by for years as I did my best to navigate and maintain friendships and strived to be the best person I could be when I went out into the world. I pressed myself to show up as kind-hearted and empathetic as possible, even when I didn't always feel my best or didn't know how to show up for others, and I did my best to understand that life is challenging for me and others around me. However, I also realize that life can get contradictory sometimes, causing us to fight between loving people despite what they do just as God does (read **Luke 17:3-4 NIV** and **Luke 23:34 NIV**), and understanding that every one who smiles in your face is not your friend, since many people also operate in the realm of hatred, jealousy, and ill will towards others. And just as in the example above, the person she thought she could trust was secretly plotting against her. Literally and figuratively trying to steal her belongings, kill her faith in humanity, and destroy the trust that once bound them to one another. But do you know that even amid turmoil, God will hide you from the secret counsel of the wicked? Think about this: As discussed in a previous section, God never said the weapons wouldn't form. But he said that they wouldn't prosper. How does that relate here?

The perpetrators attempted to steal from her, but the neighbor blocked them before they could do any significant damage. He stepped in as a hedge of protection at that moment. Just as God does when you allow him to step into your life, it doesn't mean you won't have residue, just as the broken window was residue of what could've been; however, God will send assistance so that there's no remnants of what was, similar to how that glass company was able to repair the window and make it good as new. In addition, God allowed her and her mother to leave the house before the trouble arrived. Keeping them physically safe from harm. Because if they were home, it could have been much worse. So remember that God can also physically remove you from harm's way in some situations. And lastly, remember, God hears your voice and answers your prayers. But remember, the answer doesn't always come as we think it should. Instead, the outcome can and will be opposite in most cases. For instance, when she prayed for God to remove what was not serving her friend, she knew that God would reveal something to her, but she never knew it would sever their ties. In other words, when you're praying for your friends, you never imagine God will use your exact words to remove them from your life. But you have to take it in stride, and say, **"If God didn't allow me to stay, then maybe I am in their way."** And that doesn't mean you were a bad friend, it doesn't mean you did anything wrong. Instead, it means that God is allowing THEM to walk their journey without you. In short, **everybody can't go! Even if it's YOU**! Many people say this, but I don't think they understand what they're saying. God has us walk some journeys alone so he can be the only person to get the glory out of it. But instead of questioning yourself, wondering what you could've done or said, etc., if you choose to view this as God's hiding or protection of you, it will change the entire trajectory of your life. Whether you realize it or not, God is again shielding you from the destruction they may cause to themselves or potentially YOU in the process. So, instead of forcing you to stick around and get your feelings hurt even more, he will remove you to save you. You see, when God is trying to elevate you, he will often use unconventional methods to remove any dead weight you carry, such as friendships, relationships, jobs, or anything that diverts your attention from his plan. **So, remember always to view God's redirection as his protection.** God understands that enemies will try to rise against his children, but stand firm, and know that when

you're safe in his presence, he will hide you from
all the works of iniquity[20].

---

[20] Iniquity: Refers to gross injustice or wickedness, a violation of right or duty,
or a wicked act or sin.

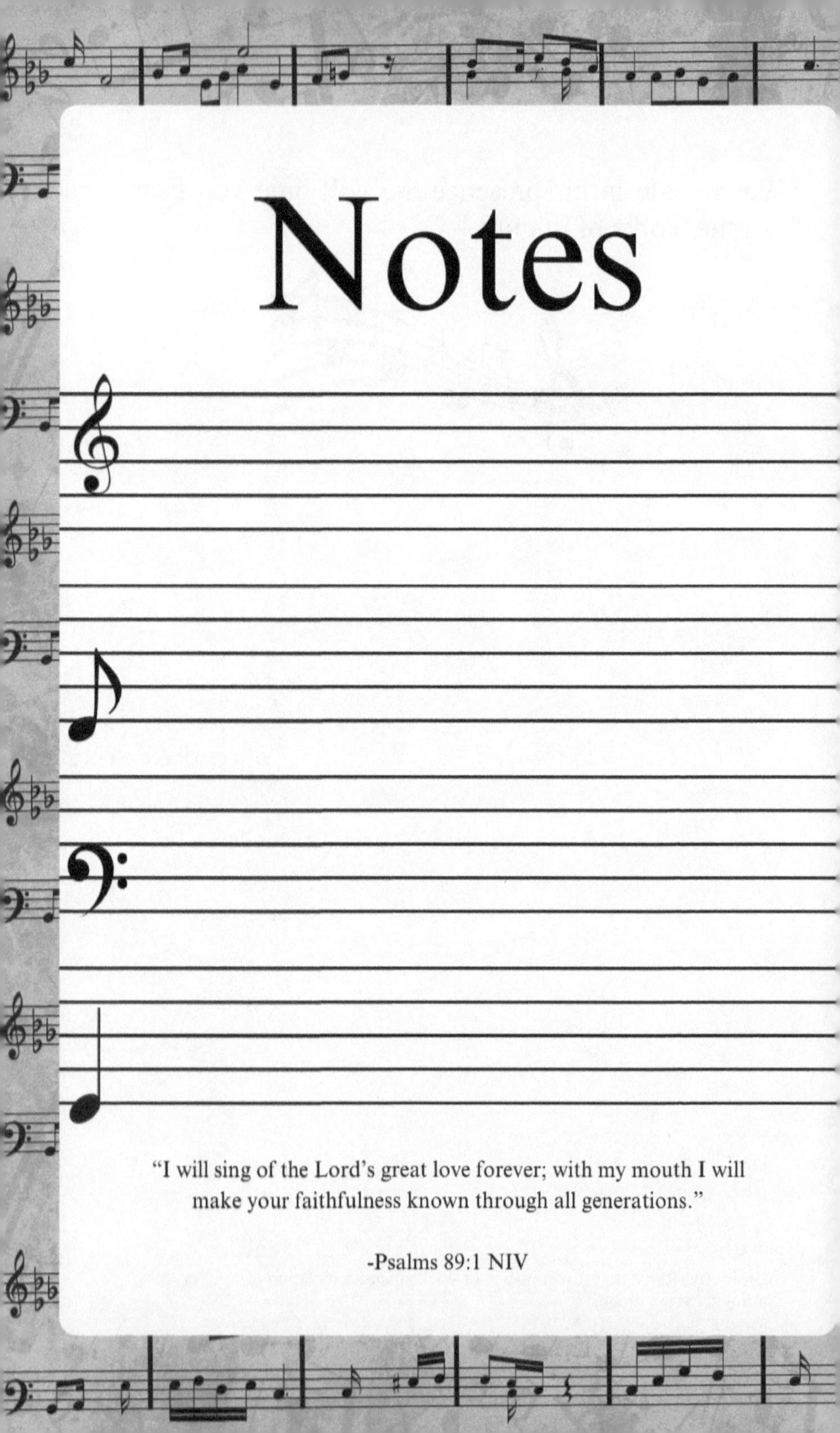

Notes
"I will sing of the Lord's great love forever; with my mouth I will make your faithfulness known through all generations."
-Psalms 89:1 NIV

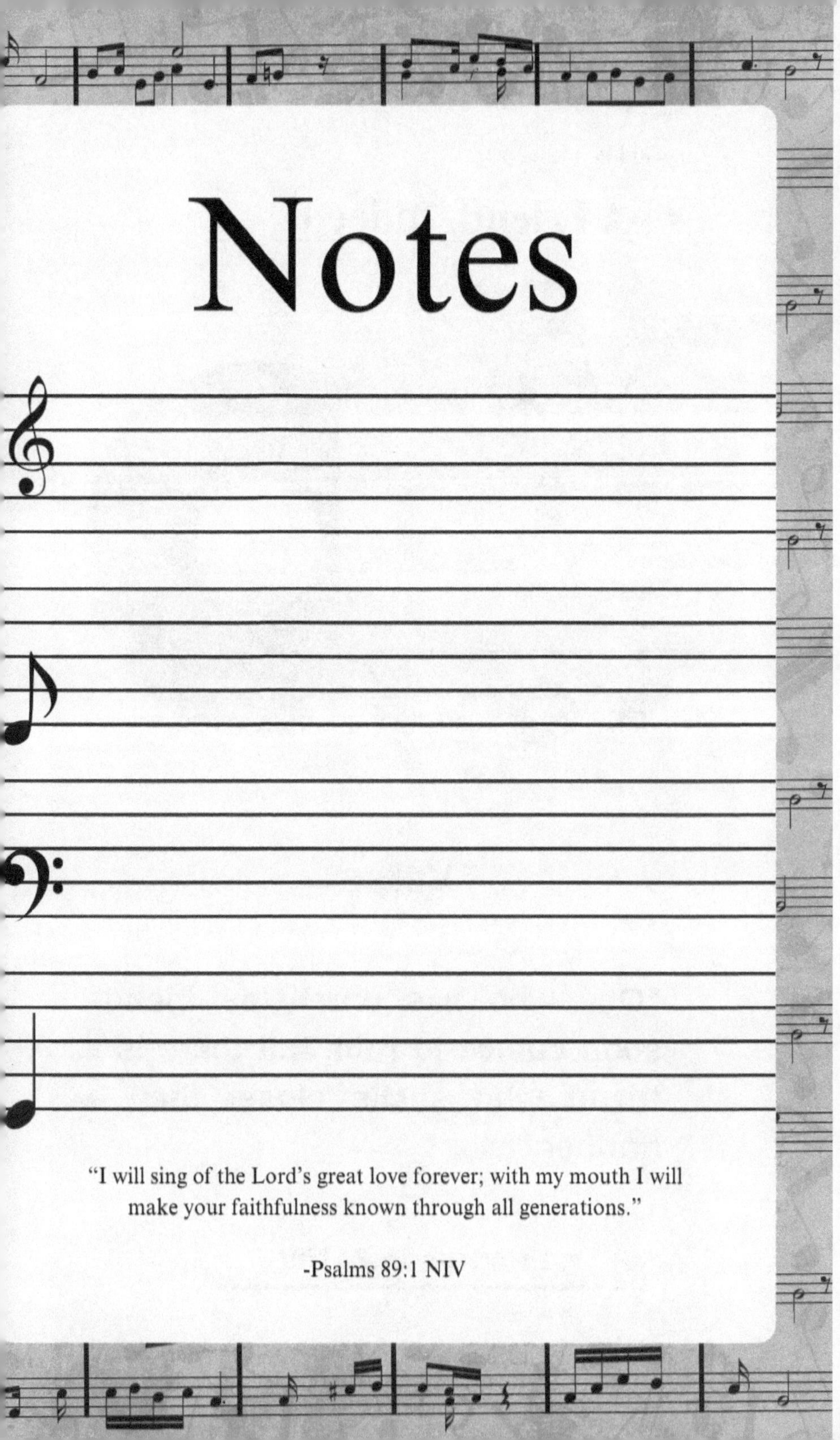

Notes
"I will sing of the Lord's great love forever; with my mouth I will make your faithfulness known through all generations."
-Psalms 89:1 NIV

A Friend, Indeed

Verse

"One who has unreliable friends soon comes to ruin, but there is a friend who sticks closer than a brother."

Proverbs 18:24 NIV

Rinngggggg! Rinngggg! Riiinngggg! The sound of my cellphone going off in the wee hours of the night. "Hello?!" I said sleepily. A soft but fragile voice on the other end of the line. "Are you asleep? I know it's late, but you're the only one I knew I could call." The room is pitch dark. The time difference is three hours ahead, as you're in Florida and they are in California. "No girl, I'm not asleep." You lied, as your conscience told you something was wrong. "What's up?! Is everything okay? You're not your usual bubbly self." Silence fills the line. "Sis, I sense something is wrong. You know you can talk to me about anything." You hear the sound of sniffling, and then a bombshell drops. "My-My grandpa, he's gone." You gasp and sit straight up in your bed. "Omg, sis! I'm so sorry! I don't even know what to say right now. All I can say is I'm sorry. I know I can't fix it, but if you need to sit on the phone and cry, I'll sit here as long as you need me to." Imagine you show up for a friend like this in their grief, and then that same person acts as if you were never there for them when they needed you the most? How would that make you feel?

Or how about this: imagine you and your friends planning to attend the concert of everyone's mutual favorite artists for months. You all looked at and priced your ideal seats and hotels, planned travel arrangements, and everything else. Still, when the week of the concert comes, everyone backs out on you, citing family emergencies and conflicting commitments as the issue. The problem is that you already purchased two tickets, and your other friend was supposed to purchase the remaining two when she got paid. Luckily, your favorite cousin gets the day off work and decides he wants to go too, so you and he choose to go together. The night is everything you hoped it would be, minus your friends being there to enjoy the moment with you: the perfect seats, view, and turn-up partner[21]. After the show, you are both on a natural high. The performance was top tier, as you already knew it would be. You and your cousin are walking back to the car, singing, dancing, and reliving all the moments. But as you get to your vehicle, something tells you to look to the left. And when you do, you see off in the distance, all of your friends together, in the parking lot, laughing and smiling. At first, you tried to give them the benefit of the doubt, *maybe they all coincidentally freed up at the last minute?* You thought to yourself. Just trying to show compassion, and not get drowned out by the slight saltiness you're feeling now. In an instant, one of your "friends" sends a text in the group chat and doesn't remove you from the thread. "We had so much fun without Veena trying

---

[21] A turn-up partner is an urban vernacular/slang term for someone who turns on the enthusiasm, gets excited, and has a good time with you, typically at a party, concert, or anywhere else that calls for a good time.

to control everything. She's so annoying. Things are much better without her around." You're fuming inside, your face visibly flustered.

"What's wrong? Why do you look like you just saw a gho-" he glances to the left and quickly back at you. Chills go down your spine. You know he saw them, but neither of you says a word. He places his arm around you, but you can't decipher whether it's to comfort you or cease you from storming over there in a rage. You show him the message on your phone. "Vee, I know it's easier said than done, but you must cut them off. They never had plans to begin with; the truth is, they lied to you. They just chose to hang out without you and weren't bold enough to say it to your face." *Buzz*, your phone vibrates. It's from one of the girls in the group chat who has now texted you separately.

"Vee, I'm so sorry. Please don't be mad at me. I love you." *Buzz*, another incoming group chat message. "Somebody had to say it! Y'all won't, but I will. I don't care how she feels." *Why wouldn't they tell me they didn't want to go with me? How long have they had animosity towards me?* You thought. *Buzz, your* phone vibrates again. But you take the high road, Veena has left the chat, and it is the last notification the group got from you. Then you blocked all parties' numbers and picked up the pieces as best as possible.

Lastly, imagine you are going to drop off your friend after a night out. You stop at a gas station because you don't have enough fuel to make it the whole route. You go inside the gas station to pay and grab a snack and a drink. "You want something, bro? I got you, get whatever you want." You ask. "Nah, bro, I'm good." He said. You approach the register, and while paying, unbeknownst to you, your friend slips a bag of chips and a candy bar into his pocket and walks out of the store ahead of you. "I'll be in the car," he says to you. "Ok, cool," you murmur as he exits the store. You can feel the once friendly demeanor of the clerk shift towards you. But you smile through it, thinking, *maybe he just had a long day?* Not realizing your friend had stolen items from the store, even after you offered to pay for them. And now you're essentially roped into something that you didn't even put yourself into in the first place. You grab your bag of items, walk to the car, get in, and pull off. As soon as you leave the gas station, you hear, *"Crumple, crunch, crumple, crunch,"* the sound of him rummaging through the chip bag. You glance at him in your peripheral vision[22], and

---

[22] Peripheral vision is the outer area/side view in your vision when you look at someone with a side view.

suddenly, the mood shifts, the looks of disapproval: it all makes sense now, you thought.

There's a popular saying, 'Birds of a feather, flock together,' which I feel is either derived from or closely related to the following scripture. "Do not be misled: 'Bad company corrupts good character" (**1 Corinthians 15:33 NIV**). Think about how often you've heard, 'watch the company you keep' or 'everyone that smiles in your face isn't your friend?' These sayings are typically warning signs when someone outside of your circle gains a bird's-eye view of the snakes that often slither around in your garden, just waiting for the right moment to attack: whether they're attacking your kindness/sincerity, your mind, your character, or your finances. Because we often lead with love when we finally find someone we can trust, **we don't usually see when someone is leeching and pretending versus when they're leading and protecting.** In other words, sometimes our grass is so high that we cannot see what lurks beneath the surface. The representative person shows can often obstruct our view of their true character. However, when we manicure our lawns (clean up our circle), we have a clearer picture of who's sincere and who's not. But in reflecting on the final example, sometimes it's too late to decide who's who? And it places you smack dab in the middle of turmoil. Which leads to the question, do birds of a feather always flock together? Or can you get swept into the flock due to your guilt by association? For example, if you don't know that your friend is stealing until after the fact, does that make you a bad person? Or is what you do next what determines the outcome? For instance, if he returns to the store and pays for the items immediately, does that mean something? Or what if he drops his friend off first, and returns to the store afterward to rectify the situation? How does he look then? On the contrary, what if the clerk doesn't accept the action, even if it's sincere? What if the clerk thinks you're lying or in on the act? Then what would you do?

You see, each of the examples above is gradual. The first one shows that you can show up for someone in the best way you know how, and it can still not be enough. You must accept that fact. The second shows that some 'friends' are only unreliable regarding you, yet they show up for others without hesitation. Those are not your friends, let them go.

And the final example proves that some 'friends' can bring you to ruin both quickly and sneakily. One wrong move, a quick stop, or a store run can change the entire trajectory of your life. The bible says, "The prudent see danger and take refuge, but the simple keep going and pay the penalty"

(Proverbs 27:12 NIV). My interpretation of this text is that those cautious in their relationships (friendships) will take refuge in the Lord. Taking refuge in the Lord, specifically, when it comes to your friends, can look different, but an example would be continuously covering oneself in prayer. Also, start praying after meeting new people, and before deciding to befriend them. Pray and wait to hear God before involving yourself fully with them. I'm not saying don't be friendly, because the word says otherwise. **Hebrews 13:2 NIV** says, "Do not forget to show hospitality to strangers, for by so doing some people have shown hospitality to angels without knowing it." However, you must walk side by side with the Lord when navigating new friendships so that you won't pay the penalty for someone else's wrongdoings. If you don't remember anything else, remember, "The righteous choose their friends carefully, but the way of the wicked leads them astray" **(Proverbs 12:26 NIV)**. **Choose wisely**.

On the contrary, if you've been blessed enough not to have friends like these, don't neglect to thank God. If you have friends who show up for you when it counts, remember to thank God for that. Thank God if you have friends who stop by when they sense something is off with you. If you have friends who don't count favors, thank God for that. And if you have friends that you don't have to second-guess, thank God for that, too, because real friends are hard to come by.

Last but not least, if you don't have anyone to call your friend, please know that a friend sticks closer than any other; his name is Jesus. And the beautiful thing is, he won't lie to you, flake on you, tell you that you're not doing enough, and lead you to the wayside like false friends do.

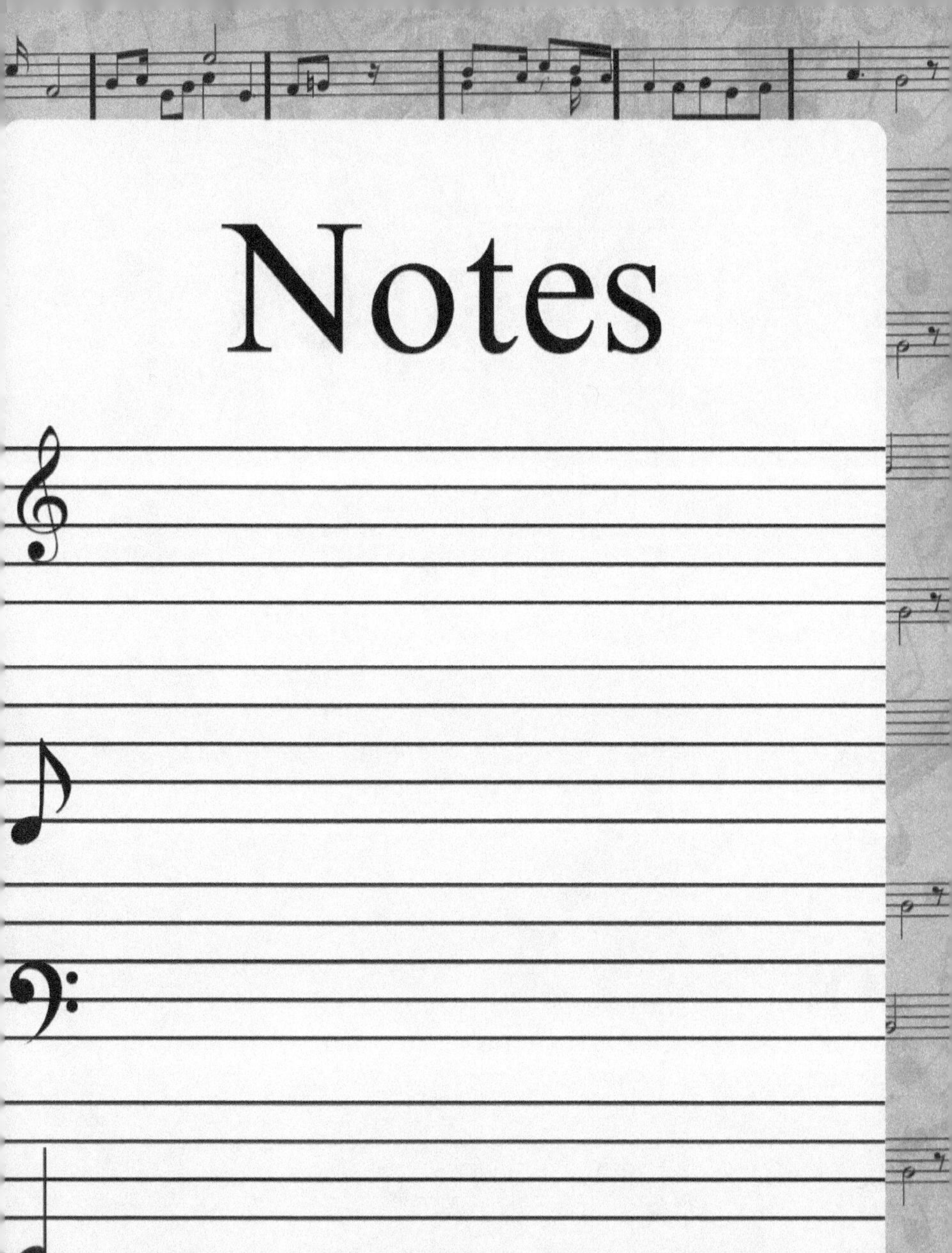

Notes

"They celebrate your abundant goodness and joyfully sing of your righteousness."

-Psalms 145:7 NIV

Notes
"They celebrate your abundant goodness and joyfully sing of your righteousness."
-Psalms 145:7 NIV

LOVE 🤍

Verses

"Dear friends, let us love one another, for love comes from God. Everyone who loves has been born of God and knows God. Whoever does not love does not know God, because God is love. This is how God showed his love among us: He sent his one and only Son into the world that we might live through him.... But perfect love drives out fear, because fear has to do with punishment. The one who fears is not made perfect in love. We love because he first loved us. Whoever claims to love God yet hates a brother or sister is a liar. For whoever does not love their brother and sister, whom they have seen, cannot love God, whom they have not seen. And he has given us this command: Anyone who loves God must also love their brother and sister." (1 John 4:7-21 NIV)

"Love is patient, love is kind. It does not envy, it does not boast, it is not proud. It does not dishonor others, it is not self-seeking, it is not easily angered, it keeps no record of wrongs. Love does not delight in evil but rejoices with the truth. It always protects, always trusts, always hopes, always perseveres. Love never fails. But where there are prophecies, they will cease; where there are tongues, they will be stilled; where there is knowledge, it will pass away." (1 Corinthians 13:4-8 NIV)

***Bonus Track: The Commodores- Jesus Is Love**

What's your definition of **Unconditional love**? Is it being accepted for who you are deep down inside, and not just your representative? Is it a person, place, or thing? A feeling? A moment forever frozen in time? A memory?

For instance, was it watching your mom exude joy while patiently waiting for you to exhaust your energy at the park, even after she worked a triple shift and had already exhausted herself? Or your dad throwing a baseball in the yard with you every Monday, Wednesday, and Friday after only getting three hours of sleep the previous night? Is it your friends showing up at your house unannounced and unprovoked, with food, drinks, and unlimited support after you announced that your dad passed away? Or is it something else? Do you have any specific example(s) that come to mind when you hear the phrase unconditional love?

It is essential to define unconditional love using real-life examples to explain what it is and is not. Unconditional love, in layperson's terms, is broken into several parts. But for time's sake, I will break it down into a few main parts. The first part is simple:

Loving without Conditions or Expectations.

In his 2018 comedy special *Tamborine*, popular comedian Chris Rock said, "Only women, children, and dogs are loved unconditionally. A man is only loved under the condition that he can provide something." And it got me thinking. That's true, to a degree. For example, imagine you've been working at your job for twenty-two years, and you come into the office and are met at the front door by your boss, who escorts you into his office. One conversation was all it took to learn your fate—a company-wide surplus ended your employment. You go home and confide in your wife; she understands and agrees to hold down the household bills until you get back on your feet. However, a year and a half later, you still have not landed a job, and your wife's finances are more scarce by the day. The more applications you submit, the more weary she becomes. "I love you, but I can't do this anymore. I need help! Financial help that you cannot provide right now." She says, deciding to call it quits.

On the contrary, let's say, your husband has been begging you for a child, and finally, after a year of trying, you conceive a son—the first child for both of you. And of course, he's excited because his first and only is a boy. And at first, he is everything you'd imagine he'd be. He helps you with daily tasks such as putting on your shoes, shaving your legs in the shower, or lifting heavy objects. He is kind, offering you words of affirmation and still telling you how beautiful you are despite how you feel as your body gradually changes, and supportive in every sense. Finally, you give birth, and everything is going smoothly. Your husband is just as supportive as he was during the pregnancy, if not more. Feeding the baby, changing the diapers, waking up in the middle of the night to soothe the baby so you can rest and recuperate, and simply dropping the gender roles by cooking, cleaning, and helping to carry the load while still loving and uplifting you. But then suddenly, a shift occurs in his demeanor towards you. He's still the perfect picture of a dad, but you feel his animosity developing towards you after a few months. And then, one day, he says flat out, "I just don't find you attractive anymore. You've gained weight since the baby, and I thought since you were breastfeeding that you would've snapped back[23] by now." You are too stunned to speak. Tears stream down your face. You swallow your pride. You're both hurt and weirdly relieved by his honesty. At least, now you know the truth.

Or, say you're a kid and your aunt has just adopted you since you're mother lost her parental rights. At first, you're excited that you don't have to go into foster care, you're under the guardianship

---

[23] To 'snap back' is a slang term for quickly returning to your original state of being / your original figure (in terms of body shape).

of someone you love and trust, and you can still see your mom on weekends. However, after only a few weeks of being under your aunt's roof, you overhear her phone conversation. "Girl, I don't want him. But that's my nephew, so I don't want to see him in the system. Plus, I need that extra income from being a foster parent. I need her to hurry up, get it together, and get her son back." In one split second, you just realized your favorite aunt doesn't feel the same way about you that you do about her, and it puts a bad taste in your mouth.

Lastly, say, your parents got you a new puppy for Christmas. You're so excited because you finally have a furry companion to call your own. You've always been an animal lover, so this is the perfect gift in your eyes. A few days after getting him, he entered your parents' closet and began chewing on your father's brand-new shoes. "Get in your cage, RIGHT NOW!" Your dad scolds her. Reluctantly, she holds her head down, whimpering and crying, and takes that slow scroll to her crate. "I knew we shouldn't have gotten this dog. It hasn't been a week yet, and she's already tearing up my shoes." You're at a crossroads. You understand how your dad feels because shoes cost money; however, you realize she's just a puppy and doesn't comprehend the value of material things.

These examples prove that men aren't the only ones who get loved conditionally: women, children, and even animals alike are also loved based on what they can provide, how they look, or how they behave. So, whether for material reasons like finances or possessions, physical reasons like weight or appearance, or for control purposes, we all have experienced love based on our current condition or a particular expectation that we are supposed to uphold. And whenever we don't, man[24] restricts the love we can or cannot receive. However, the beautiful thing about God is that we don't have to do or be anything for him to accept us. God loves us as we are—no strings attached.

The second part is **Love Without Judgement.**

Say you're overworked and overwhelmed, working nonstop as a criminal defense attorney with minimal sleep. You drive down a long stretch of road on your way home. *Only five minutes left*, you thought. Your eyes get heavier, Skurrtttt! Boom! You closed your eyes briefly, hit a pothole, lost wheel control, and swerved off the road. In an instant, you hit an innocent pedestrian who was on the sidewalk and in the process of crossing the street. "Omg! Omg! Hello, operator, I need an ambulance." You turn on your hazard lights and

---

[24] In this case, the term "man" is not gender specific

swiftly get out of the car, coming to the aid of the pedestrian, who's fully alert, and balled up on the concrete, cradling her arm.

Hypothetically speaking, say she remained by the side of the pedestrian until the rescue came, took care of all of the medical expenses associated, and accepted whatever consequences came her way. And to her surprise, by the grace of God, the pedestrian says, "I'm not pressing charges. I saw the whole thing unfold, and there was no way she could safely avoid the pothole without swerving off the side of the road. I thought I had more time. I could chance it, and I darted out in front of her vehicle before she could come to a complete stop." After examination, they determined that the pedestrian was okay, and besides a minor sprain in her arm and a few scrapes, she was the perfect picture of health. *Thank God she's OK,* you thought. Still shaken up by the whole ordeal, but doing your best to stand tall. You exchanged contact information with the pedestrian, and after everything was all over, the two of you developed a solid and lasting friendship. Which begs the question? Would you have the heart to forgive, empathize with, and befriend someone who put you in harm's way, whether intentionally or not? **Could you testify to save a person's life who almost cost you your own?** If you answered no, you may not operate in a judgment-free mindset like you think you do. Loving without judgment means that regardless of what someone does to you, no matter how hurtful, dangerous, or potentially life-altering, you must walk in love and forgiveness just as Christ does with us. Take a moment to ponder all of the close calls you've had in your life. Have you escaped things you thought you'd pay the consequences for because God allowed an angel on earth to come to your defense? Have you ever sat back and counted all the times you could've been judged and humiliated, yet God gave you a clean slate? What does that tell you about God's love for you and the love you must exhibit for others around you?

The third part is **Accepting People As They Are.**

"Sweetie, any update on your mom's ETA? I have an appointment in a few!" The attendant at the Boys and Girls Club said as she locked the main door to the building. You sit outside on the curb, the last child standing, as everyone else's parents have already come and gone. *Mama hasn't been on time to pick me up for the third time.* You snap out of it. "I tried calling her several times, but she didn't answer." She turns her head, rolls her eyes, and sighs softly to hide her aggravation. "Here, use my phone and try your mom again?" Finally, she answers, words slurring. "Hello!? May I ask whose calling?" There's a slight pause. "Mom, it's me.

Where are you? The Boys and Girls Club is closed already. I'm the only one-" Your mother gasps, "Omg! Honey, I'm sorry. I overslept. Be there in 10." *Click,* she hangs up the phone. You had the call on speaker, so the attendant heard every word. *She didn't oversleep. I know she's lying; she's slurring.* You're deep in your thoughts. Your mom must've driven a hundred miles an hour to get to you because she was pulling up in the blink of an eye. She emerges from the car apologetic to the attendant, her hair frizzy, alcohol permeating through her pores, and her eyes bloodshot red, the same color as her lipstick. She could barely walk straight from the car to the curb, but your eyes lit up when you saw her, and vice versa. "Thank you, ma'am, for waiting with me." You give the attendant a brief hug. And take off running into your mother's arms, "Mommy, I missed you!" She kisses your forehead, "I missed you too, honey, let's go home."

I don't know about you, but if you've ever loved someone through addictions like alcoholism, you know that it is the embodiment of loving them and accepting them as they are, even if it's to your detriment[25]. For instance, as a child of a parent with an addiction, you often feel a combination of love, shame, and constant worry. Singled out as the

---

[25] Detriment is about something causing you harm or damage

child of a person with an addiction. You must always over-explain and over-compensate for actions that are not your own, such as constant tardiness, slurring words, loud outbursts, and stumbling. On the other hand, you're scared that today will be 'that' day, the one where she won't be there to pick you up ever again. Afraid that her life, your life, and the lives of others hang in her hands. So you run into her arms every time you see her and hug her a little tighter each time, so that while you still have her in the flesh, you can have the memories of loving her with every fiber of your being and cherishing the time you share because our time on earth is limited. Don't believe me? Well, the Bible says, "Why, you do not even know what will happen tomorrow. What is your life? You are a mist that appears for a little while and then vanishes."(**James 4:14 NIV**) To put it plainly, all of our lives are temporary. One minute we're here, and the next we vanish. So, knowing that her life is precious, and yours too, you choose to love and accept her exactly as she is, just as God accepts you exactly the way you are!

The final part is **Forgiveness of Offenses.**

The most critical form of unconditional love is the forgiveness of offenses. The Bible says, "Bear with each other and forgive one another if any of you has a grievance against someone. Forgive as the Lord forgave you." **(Colossians 3:13 NIV)**[26] We as humans tend to harbor hatred and anger towards others, yet we want God to shower us with love, understanding, and forgiveness when we refuse to do the same for his other children. But it doesn't work that way. In short, we have to give forgiveness to get forgiveness. We cannot keep score of the wrongdoings. Instead, we must clear the scoreboard to walk in the steadfast love God has in store for us.

Now, imagine you just discovered that your spouse had been cheating on you for the entire duration of the seven years you've been married and had a secret love child, a son, with his mistress. "So let me get this straight, you've been lying, cheating, and you have a whole other child that you hid from me, and your other kids? Why would you do this to me? To them?" The tears won't stop flowing. "I'm sorry, baby, I don't know what I was thinking. Please forgive me." You sigh. "It's not that simple. You had no regard for me this whole time. You put my life and health at risk by sleeping with her and then coming back and sleeping with me. That's so nasty and low down." He tries to grab your hand, but you swat his hand away. "I don't think I can do this anymore, Apollo. I love you and forgive you, but I can't stick around

---

[26] Also, see Matthew 6:14-15 NIV, Ephesians 6:42 NIV, & 1 John 1:9 NIV

and let you continue to hurt me." You turn to walk away, but you ask him one last question before you do.

"I'm going to leave to clear my head for the night, but before I do, I'm just curious how old your son is?" He hesitates. "H-He's five!" *Five! The same age as our youngest? Wow! It keeps getting worse!* You thought. "Well, now that it's all out in the open, can the kids meet? They're siblings, so there's no point in shielding them from one another now." His eyes widen. "Call her and tell her I want to meet with her. We need to have a conversation and get on one accord."

In this example, you see the ultimate display of betrayal after a wife discovers her husband has been unfaithful to her throughout their marriage and has had a love child the same age as their youngest son. However, she displays forgiveness in a few different ways. First, she verbally says, "I love you and I forgive you, but I won't let you hurt me." You see, walking in forgiveness does not mean that you have to allow someone back into your life, but it does mean that you don't keep a record of the offense. Since children are often caught in the crossfire of adult situations, taking the initiative not to shield them from one another and allowing them to have a relationship is an ultimate act of acceptance and forgiveness. And finally, the effort to get on one accord with his mistress, so the family doesn't miss a beat. That is the ultimate display of selflessness and love because it takes a strong woman to forgive your spouse, his mistress, and not hold any animosity towards the children that are not your own.

These examples show us that walking in forgiveness is tough sometimes. Truthfully, it's messy and occasionally conflicting because we often want to walk in flesh when someone offends us, but God tells us the contrary. So every ill action done to us, regardless of how devastating, gut-wrenching, or deceitful, must be fully forgiven and covered in grace for us to walk in true unconditional love like Christ does. The word says, "Whoever does not love does not know God, because God is love." (**1 John 4:8 NIV**).

In sum, if you want to know what true love is, seek the source (God) and allow his love to be exhibited daily through you. Love is a beautiful thing, don't let anyone tell you otherwise. The truth is that most people who speak against love have no genuine concept of what love is. And most of those people have a void in their heart where God should be. So, be careful not to miss out on a life with him at the center, because a life without him is a life without true LOVE, and let's face it, who truly wants to live a life void of the love that Christ displays for us all. I know I don't, but what about you? Do you want to be filled? If so, seek his face and ask him to fill that void in your heart with the unconditional love that only he can fill you with. And don't be afraid, for "this is good, and pleases God our Savior, who wants all people to be saved and to come to a knowledge of the truth." **(1 Timothy 2:3-4 NIV)**

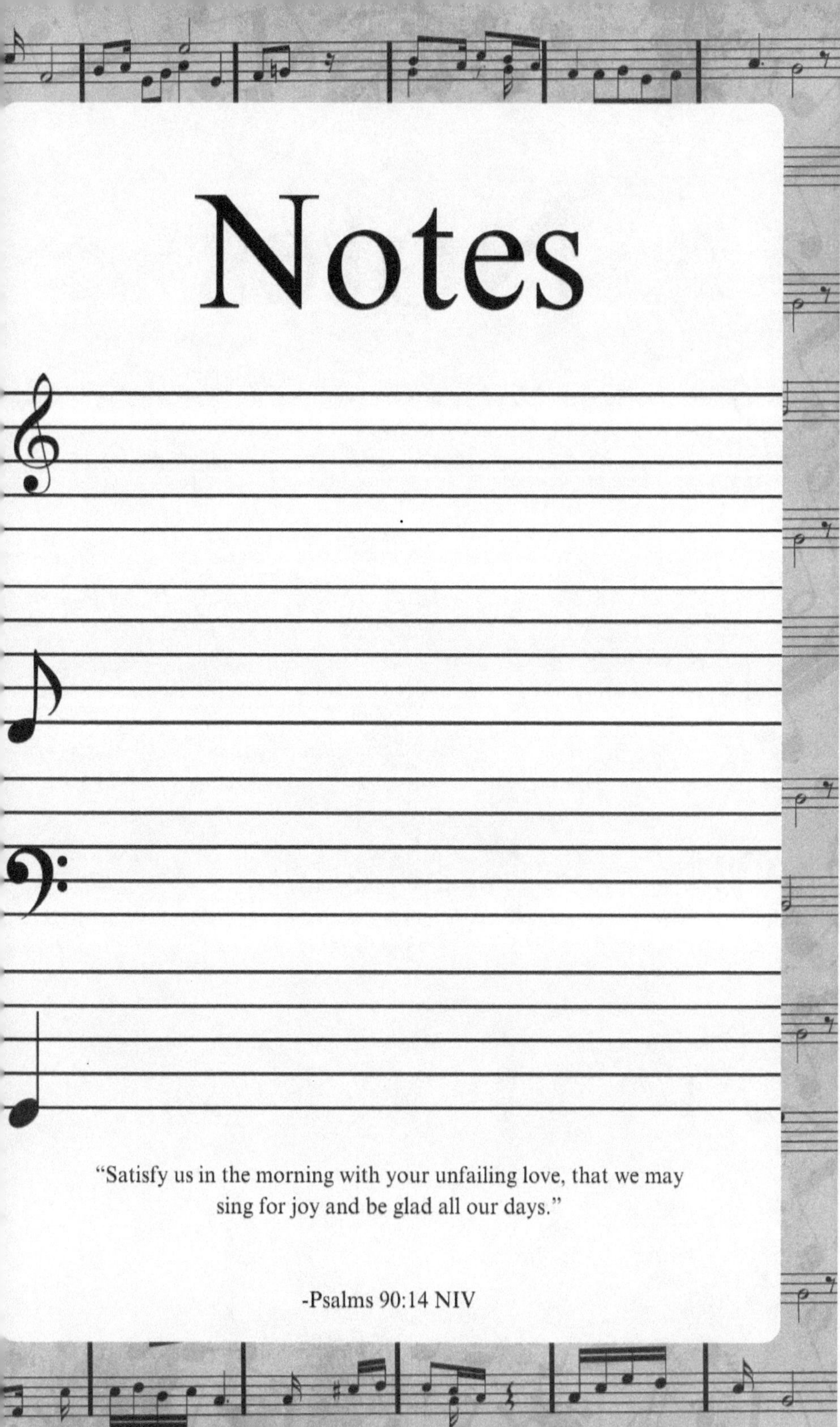

Notes

"Satisfy us in the morning with your unfailing love, that we may
sing for joy and be glad all our days."

-Psalms 90:14 NIV

Notes

"Satisfy us in the morning with your unfailing love, that we may
sing for joy and be glad all our days."

-Psalms 90:14 NIV

Outro

"Let the message of Christ dwell among you richly as you teach and admonish one another with all wisdom through psalms, hymns, and songs from the Spirit, singing to God with gratitude in your hearts. And whatever you do, whether in word or deed, do it all in the name of the Lord Jesus, giving thanks to God the Father through him." **(Colossians 3:16-17 NIV)**

Scan to listen

TO BE

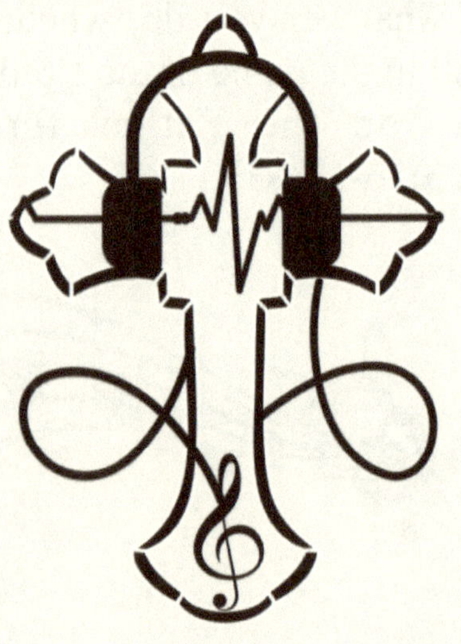

CONTINUED...

About the Author

Brittany Thomas is the author of Saving (This Song For) You Vol. 1, which is the freshman installment of this series. She is a writer/ author, pastry artist/entrepreneur (Sug'r Rush), a self-proclaimed podcaster (Spill'n Honey Podcast) & Food Critic, and an all-around creative. She holds a BA in English: Editing, Writing & Media (Florida State University) and an MA in Creative Writing with a concentration in Screenwriting from Southern New Hampshire University. She is a native of Jacksonville, Florida. She loves traveling, listening to music, and sleeping (whenever that happens, lol).

Credits

"Beau." *Merriam-Webster.com*. Merriam-Webster, 2011.Web. Accessed 25 May 2025.

"Deflect." *Merriam-Webster.com*. Merriam-Webster, 2011.Web. Accessed 25 May 2025.

"Detriment." *Merriam-Webster.com*. Merriam-Webster, 2011.Web. Accessed 25 May 2025.

"Dilation and Curettage (D&C) - Mayo Clinic." *Mayo Clinic*, 7 Nov. 2023, www.mayoclinic.org/tests-procedures/dilation-and-curettage/about/pac-20384910. Accessed 25 May 2025.

"Flex." *Merriam-Webster.com*. Merriam-Webster, 2011.Web. Accessed 25 May 2025.

"Forestalling." *Merriam-Webster.com*. Merriam-Webster, 2011.Web. Accessed 25 May 2025.

"Forbade." *Merriam-Webster.com*. Merriam-Webster, 2011.Web. Accessed 25 May 2025.

"Fret." *Merriam-Webster.com*. Merriam-Webster, 2011.Web. Accessed 25 May 2025.

"Gripe." *Merriam-Webster.com*. Merriam-Webster, 2011.Web. Accessed 25 May 2025.

"Iniquity." *Merriam-Webster.com*. Merriam-Webster, 2011.Web. Accessed 25 May 2025.

"Intercept." *Merriam-Webster.com*. Merriam-Webster, 2011.Web. Accessed 25 May 2025.

"Loom." cambridge.org/dictionary. © Cambridge University Press & Assessment 2025. Web. Accessed 25 May 2025.

"Merciful" *Merriam-Webster.com*. Merriam-Webster, 2011.Web. Accessed 25 May 2025.

"Oblige" *Merriam-Webster.com*. Merriam-Webster, 2011.Web. Accessed 25 May 2025.

"Official Rule Book: Technical Rules." *USA Boxing*, 1 Jan. 2014, d36m266ykvepgv.cloudfront.net/uploads/media/ QblZ66O15c/o/usa-boxing-technical-rules-8-9-13.pdf. Accessed 25 May 2025.

"Omnibenevolent, Adj." Oxford English Dictionary, Oxford UP, December 2024, https:// doi.org/10.1093/OED/1953960912. Web. Accessed 25 May 2025.

"Omnipresent." *Merriam-Webster.com*. Merriam-Webster, 2011.Web. Accessed 25 May 2025.

"Peripheral." *Merriam-Webster.com*. Merriam-Webster, 2011.Web. Accessed 25 May 2025.

"Shadow" *Merriam-Webster.com*. Merriam-Webster, 2011.Web. Accessed 25 May 2025.

"Snap Back" *Merriam-Webster.com*. Merriam-Webster, 2011.Web. Accessed 25 May 2025.

"Turn-Up" *UrbanDictionary.com*. Urban Dictionary, ©1999-2025.Web. Accessed 25 May 2025.
Tambourine. Rock, Chris. Dir. Bo Burnham, Prod. Neal Brennan, Jax Media, 2014. Netflix. Accessed 25 May 2025.

The Holy Bible. American Standard Version® (ASV). *YouVersion*, app version 10.21.0, Copyright © 2020. Used by permission. All rights reserved. Accessed 25 May 2025.

The Holy Bible. English Standard Version® (ESV). *YouVersion*, app version 10.21.0, Copyright © 2016, by Crossway / Good News Publishers.®, Used by permission. All rights reserved. Accessed 25 May 2025.

The Holy Bible, New International Version® (NIV), *YouVersion*, app version 10.21.0, Copyright © 1973, 1978, 1984, 2011 by Biblica, Inc.®, Used by permission. All rights reserved. Accessed 25 May 2025.

The Holy Bible. New Living Translation® (NLT). *YouVersion*, app version 10.21.0, Tyndale House Publishers Inc.®, Copyright © 1996, 2004, 2007, 2013. Used by permission. All rights reserved. Accessed 25 May 2025.

"Unscathed" *Merriam-Webster.com*. Merriam-Webster, 2011. Web. Accessed 25 May 2025.
"Vigilant." *Merriam-Webster.com*. Merriam-Webster, 2011. Web. Accessed 25 May 2025.

"Washing Your Hands." *Dictionary.com*. Dictionary.com, LLC, 2025. Web. Accessed 25 May 2025.
"Wretch." *Merriam-Webster.com*. Merriam-Webster, 2011. Web. Accessed 25 May 2025.

Commodores. "Jesus Is Love." *All The Great Love Songs*, Motown, 1984, https://youtu.be/8oWlg3-iIiE?si=KbdjLsO1tLZQD20V. Youtube. Accessed 25 May 2025.

Crouch, Andraé & Winans, Marvin. "Let The Church Say Amen." *The Journey*, Riverphlo Entertainment, 2011, https://youtu.be/sZKA2iY9ATA?si=pOQ12p773Z-tDYEZ. Youtube. Accessed 25 May 2025.

Franklin, Kirk. "Father Knows Best." *Long Live Love*, Fo Yo Soul Recordings & RCA Records, a division of Sony Music Entertainment, 2019, https://youtu.be/j6DZ_RVHTzo?si=hDVxfpt-JkuYtiaQ. Youtube. Accessed 25 May 2025.

God's Property & Franklin, Kirk. "Love." *God's Property From Kirk Franklin's Nu Nation*, GospoCentric, Interscope, 1997, https://youtu.be/wazZoA4CnqA?si=tpxHBfYhzifcSDO0. Youtube. Accessed 25 May 2025.

Hammond, Fred & Radicals for Christ. "No Weapon." *Spirit of David,* New Spring Publishing Inc., Kassner Associated Publishers Ltd., K & F Music, St Swithin's Songs, New Spring Publishing Inc., St Swithin S Songs, 1996, https://youtu.be/

n_L77bD5WYg?si=dZF_iXZpvFQLr2p3.
Youtube. Accessed 25 May 2025.

Houghton, Israel & New Breed. "Friend of God."
Decade, Integrity's Praise! Music, 2000, https://
youtu.be/JRGOleYc4sE?
si=VU2tVkjCOYoGLyBJ. YouTube. Accessed 25
May 2025.

Houston, Whitney & The Georgia Mass Choir. "I
Love The Lord." *The Preacher's Wife Original
Soundtrack Album,* Published by Richwood
Music / Century Oak Publishing Group, adm. by
CMI (BMI), 1996, https://youtu.be/iPLP1ui4YNc?
si=WhYWBQhuCeLdCLv9. Youtube. Accessed
25 May 2025.

Mann, Tamela. "Change Me." *One Way*, Tillymann
Inc., 2016, https://youtu.be/rSM96kWKg1s?
si=aggOdyKakcdyhYmE. Youtube. Accessed 25
May 2025.

McClurkin, Donnie. "Great Is Your Mercy (Live)."
Live In London And More, Zomba Recordings
LLC., 2000, https://youtu.be/y-bh2TO8lMM?
si=f0h89CPeYJ0R1eGo. Youtube. Accessed 25
May 2025.

McClurkin, Donnie & Tribbett, Tye. "We Are
Victorious." *Duets*, Don Mac Music, 2014, https://

youtu.be/OIun53iz6s4?si=HSo0Ozkb6oIyi6fb.
Youtube. Accessed 25 May 2025.

Munizzi, Martha. "I Know The Plans." *The Best Is Yet To Come*, Say The Name Publishing, 2003, https://youtu.beja2XaS_JeDk? si=eX0GyHC6ykX7K-s9. YouTube. Accessed 25 May 2025.

Murphy, William & Morton, Bishop James. "Everlasting God." *Demonstrate (Deluxe Edition),* RCA Records, a division of Sony Music Entertainment, 2016, https://youtu.be/ qQlDLMaWHQA?si=SZbBE_EakLHNE_oU. YouTube. Accessed 25 May 2025.

Norful, Smokie. "Psalm 64." *I Need You Now*, EMI Gospel, 2002, https://youtu.be/ AGLuDyZYHHg?si=xVU0dnxpfrX2GAZr. YouTube. Accessed 25 May 2025.

Sheard-Clark, Karen. "A Secret Place." *2nd Chance*, Elektra Records, 2002, https://youtu.be/ Arpe-DdVY10?si=jCuGmzr1E0td1kph. YouTube. Accessed 25 May 2025.

Silk, Garnett. "Splashing Dashing." Give I Strength, 2003 VP Music Group, 1999, https:// youtu.be/SaxQchd1wtw?si=aLyd0lDBmTRRyS1f. YouTube. Accessed 25 May 2025.

Studdard, Ruben. "Amazing Grace." I Need An Angel, 19 Recordings Limited, 2004, https://youtu.be/QCdFi0Kwf3Q?si=QZ9grNRjbIb9IInh. YouTube. Accessed 25 May 2025.